A NO-STRINGS NOEL

ANNABELLE JACOBS

CHAPTER 1

"Do it like you mean it, big boy! That's it, right there."

Henry stood in the doorway to his boyfriend's bedroom, not sure whether to laugh or cry. "Well, this is awkward."

"*Fuck.*" Kyle, his boyfriend of six months, currently dick-deep in—Henry leant to the side to get a better look—ahh, Mika from next door, glanced back at him with a look of shock. But, Henry noted with a weird sort of detachment, he didn't stop ploughing into Mika, just slowed his pace to a leisurely stroke instead of a rabid jackhammer. "You're back early."

"I am." Henry raised an eyebrow and gestured to the bed. "And *for fuck's sake*, can you get your dick out of Mika for five fucking minutes while I'm trying to talk to you?"

Kyle had the nerve to sigh as he pulled out and slumped to the side, facing Henry.

He still had the fucking condom on.

"Jesus." Henry scrubbed a hand over his eyes, having seen enough. He should've been full of rage, ready to give Kyle a piece of his mind, but all he felt was numb. No words waited to spill out. In fact, his mind was sort of blank.

I need to get out of here.

Henry's pyjama bottoms lay on the floor where he'd left them a couple of hours ago, and an unexpected bark of laughter burst out. "I bet the bed wasn't even cold. Did you even bother to have a shower after we fucked this morning?"

Kyle shrugged and Mika turned over to glare at him. "Really? You couldn't have had a fucking wash before I came over?"

That's all he's bothered about?

Henry was done.

So fucking done.

And so were he and Kyle.

"Box up my stuff. I'll come round to collect it at the weekend."

"Henry, wait, this doesn't mean anything."

Henry grimaced. "Oh, so you weren't *doing it like you meant it,* then? *Big boy.*"

Mika snorted and Kyle went to get up, but Henry shot his hand out.

"Don't bother. I'm leaving. We're finished, Kyle." He turned and walked away, ignoring Kyle shouting his name.

It wasn't until he got outside that it all hit him.

With shaking hands, Henry unlocked his car and slid behind the wheel. "Shit," he whispered, eyes filling with tears. Six months wasn't ages, but Henry had liked him.

A lot.

And being cheated on was the fucking worst.

His gut told him it wasn't the first time either. Before his mind could wander down that path, Henry pulled out his phone and messaged his sister.

Henry: You home?

Ella: Yes, why?

Henry: Caught K fucking someone else.

Ella: THAT NASTY LITTLE CUNT. I HOPE HE CATCHES HIS FORESKIN IN HIS ZIP.

Henry smiled despite himself.

Henry: Such a way with words.

Ella: I try.

Ella: I'm getting out the ice cream and the vodka.

Henry: Be there in five.

ONE PINT OF BEN & Jerry's Phish Food and half a bottle of vodka later, Henry sat slumped on his sister's sofa, cradling a shot glass. "Why?" he mused, reaching for the bottle.

Ella scoffed and held out her glass for a refill. "Because he's a weasel-dicked little arsehole." She clinked her glass against Henry's and gently nudged his shoulder. "And he obviously didn't deserve you."

Henry rolled his eyes. "Because I'm *obviously* such a catch."

"You are." Ella turned in her seat to glare at him with slightly unfocused eyes. Or maybe it was Henry's that were unfocused.

"I'm twenty-six, almost twenty-seven, and I still live with my uni mates. I work at Tesco, for fuck's sake."

"Hey." Ella waved her now-empty glass at him. "Only because you haven't found your forever job yet. And there's nothing wrong with working at Tesco. You never used to think like that until Kyle-the-arsehole kept taking the piss."

True.

Ella relieved him of the bottle and poured another shot. "At least you don't have to worry about driving round mountains and going on ski lifts now."

"What?" It took Henry's booze-addled brain a moment to parse her words.

Oh.

The skiing trip.

Kyle's early Christmas present to Henry had been a skiing trip at the end of November. He'd paid for everything. All Henry had to do was provide his own spending money. Which he'd picked up extra shifts to save for.

On the surface, it seemed a wonderful gesture his boyfriend had made. Except Henry was frightened of heights.

Terrified, to be more precise.

He didn't like walking next to the glass barrier on the top floor of the shopping centre.

A fact Kyle had rolled his eyes at and promptly ignored.

A shudder ran through him at the thought of the bus ride to the resort. "I read online that some of the roads have sheer drops."

Ella shook her head. "I still can't believe he booked it after you told him you're afraid of heights."

"He said it would do me good to face my fears."

She poured them another drink and pointed the bottle at Henry. "And why the hell did you agree to go, anyway?"

He sighed and slumped back against the sofa cushions. "I wanted to make him happy."

Ella's pitying look wasn't something he could deal with right then, so he waved a hand at her. "Get rid of that face. It doesn't matter now." He downed his shot, wincing at the burn and the slight protest from his stomach. Tomorrow would be brutal. "I'm not going skiing with Kyle or doing anything with him ever again."

Ella raised her glass. "I'll drink to that."

Henry laughed at her but then shook his head. "Instead, I get to spend a week at home doing fuck all. Again."

Fear of heights aside, the idea of getting away for a bit had been something he'd looked forward to. It felt like forever since he'd done that. "I guess I could always cancel my time off and go into work instead." Not an appealing thought either.

"Oh!" Ella sat up straight and set the vodka bottle down with a clang. "I've just had the best idea."

Henry narrowed his eyes, knowing from experience Ella's drunken ideas never worked out well for him. "No. Whatever it is, just no."

"You've not even heard it yet." She grabbed her phone, and after a couple of attempts at typing something, sat back with a satisfied smile. "Now we wait for him to reply."

"Who? And about what?" He nudged her with his foot. "What have you done?"

"Stop looking so moody. I'm trying to sort out a holiday for you."

Henry frowned and ran a hand through his hair, massaging his temple where a headache threatened. "I can sort out my own holiday, El."

Her phone buzzed and she snatched it up off the coffee table, her smile widening as she read. "No need. It's done. And it'll only cost you about two hundred quid for the week."

"That sounds suspiciously cheap." Where the fuck was she sending him? "I'm not spending a week in a freezing caravan somewhere. I'd rather stay at home, thanks."

"It's not a caravan, and you won't need to drive all that far either." She made her eyes wide and gave him that look. The one that spelt trouble and, unfortunately, the one he couldn't say no to. "Do you trust me?"

He slung his arm around her shoulder and pulled her into his side. "You know I do."

"Then believe me when I say you'll enjoy this. I know you don't mind being on your own, so this is perfect."

Knowing he was most likely going to regret this, but having had far too much vodka to care, Henry nodded. "Okay, fine." Ella clapped her hands and snatched her phone up to type a message back to whoever she'd been chatting with.

"Right, so, three weeks on Friday, you'll be going here." She held up her phone triumphantly, showing him the website for a family holiday park, and Henry groaned. "Their Christmas decorations go up throughout the park next week. It'll be *so* festive." She laughed. "Even you won't be able to resist getting in the Christmas spirit."

"It's not even December yet." Not that Henry was averse to Christmas or anything, but he didn't normally go mad with it like Ella. And he doubted he'd be feeling the urge to celebrate, considering he'd just broken up with his boyfriend.

"Have you already forgotten that I'm heartbroken?"

That wiped the smile off her face and Henry instantly felt guilty. "I'm sorry. I keep forgetting that you're upset about it all, whereas I couldn't be happier."

Henry snorted. She'd never hidden the fact she thought Kyle was a knob. Turned out she'd been right after all.

"Just go away for the week, enjoy the crisp fresh air and pamper yourself. They have a huge spa, massive swimming area, and lots of restaurants. And you can walk to your heart's content."

"But it's a *family* place." Henry liked children well enough, but being surrounded by them whilst holidaying alone wasn't his idea of fun.

"It's not even the school holidays. How many kids can there be?" The way she wouldn't look him in the eye as she said it told him all he needed to know.

Arse.

I'm never drinking vodka again.

NOVEMBER 26TH

Henry thanked the very nice lady at the check-in booth as she handed him his villa keys and a map, then he followed the arrows to the massive car park. Apparently he couldn't go into his one-bed villa until 4pm, but he could enjoy the rest of the facilities that the holiday park had to offer. Which he had to admit after looking them up online were an impressive amount.

They'd spared no expense on their festive holiday decorations either. The long winding road through the forest had been littered with LED animals and trees.

Even Henry was starting to feel Christmassy.

But going anywhere new unsettled him until he'd got his bearings, so with more than a little trepidation, Henry parked up, grabbed his rucksack, and headed in the direction that everyone else seemed to be going.

He'd arrived early. Might as well get his money's worth, after all. But the car park was already packed.

And despite his sister's assurances to the contrary, there *were* kids.

Lots of kids.

Pre-school age ones.

Henry sighed. He really needed to get over himself.

Kids were fine.

You like them. Usually.

You're still pissed off over Kyle and everything is annoying at the moment.

The reception arrows seemed like a good thing to follow, and Henry trudged along with everyone else until the massive dome came into view.

Ahh, that'll be the pool area.

It was a lot bigger than he'd anticipated.

Once he walked through the sliding doors, he saw why. It needed to accommodate the fucking huge Christmas tree that greeted everyone as they came in. Henry had to tilt his head back a little to see the top of it. Shops and restaurants lined the sides of a wide, festively decorated pathway that curved round and down.

And it was hot, too.

He'd expected it to be warmer than the outside, obviously, but this was a warm, sticky heat that was rapidly making him uncomfortable.

It was also busy.

Really busy.

Henry wasn't sure he could cope with this many people for the next seven days.

As he took off his gloves and his beanie, he looked around for somewhere to sit while he worked out what to do for the next six hours.

Six hours.

Jeez.

I'm going to kill Ella for this.

"Hi."

Henry looked up and immediately froze when he met a pair of startling green eyes staring back at him. The square jaw and accompanying warm smile made his brain go offline for a second, and much to his horror he couldn't make his mouth work.

The guy was about an inch or so taller than Henry, with big wide shoulders and hair the colour of straw.

He was attractive in that rugged kind of way that made Henry imagine him working outdoors with his hands.

The guy held out one of those hands towards Henry. "I'm Dom."

Manners made Henry automatically reach out and accept the handshake. "Henry."

Dom smiled wryly. "I don't often accost strangers in the reception area, but you looked kind of lost and confused."

Henry laughed. "I am." No point denying it when even complete strangers could see it.

"First time?"

"I'm sorry?"

Dom chuckled. "Coming here. Is this the first time you've been?"

"Yes." Henry glanced around the busy reception area, at restaurants and cafes with every available seat taken, and shuddered. "You're telling me people actually come back for more?"

"It's only like this on changeover days. On a Monday and Friday, everyone gets kicked out of their villas by ten, and you have all the new people coming in, so it gets a bit busy."

"A bit?"

"Well, all the Christmas decorations are up now, so that adds to it, I guess. But it'll be a lot quieter from tomorrow."

"Mm-hmm."

"Trust me. I come here a lot."

Henry wanted to ask, *why would you do that?* but decided that would probably be rude. "Okay, I have just under six hours before I can get in my villa. What do you suggest I do until then, since you're such an expert?" he asked instead and winced at his tone. "Sorry. Didn't mean to sound like a twat." He waved at the people around them. "I'm not keen on crowds."

Dom shrugged. "Who is?" He went to put his hand on Henry's arm, then looked up. "Can I?"

Henry nodded, a little amazed. The first time he'd met Kyle, he'd manhandled Henry up against the bar without even asking his name first.

With a gentle touch, Dom guided him over to a display board that housed a map of the park and photos of various activities. "On changeover days, the dome area gets really busy, especially when the weather is shit. So the pool is out, and so are the restaurants unless you've pre-booked. But the pool gets a lot emptier between three thirty and four thirty while all the newbies rush to get into their villas."

"Good to know." Henry would most likely be one of those newbies.

Dom pointed to the lake on the map. "You've got the sports area down there. The bar and café are probably just as busy as up here, but the sports facilities are usually okay if you want to book a badminton or tennis court."

"It won't be much fun playing with myself." Henry laughed, then immediately flushed when he realised what he'd said.

Dom cocked an eyebrow. "I quite enjoy playing with myself. Although doing it with a partner is preferable, I agree."

Henry stared at him, opening his mouth, then shutting it again before letting out words that had no business leaving his lips. "And, um . . . will your partner be joining you soon?" *Omg Henry, you've only just met the man.*

The sudden silence seemed to last an age as Dom studied his face, and Henry mentally crossed his fingers that his lame attempt at flirting hadn't landed him in trouble.

Dom finally sighed as though deciding something and ran a hand through his hair. "My partner and I were supposed to be coming here together, but we're no longer a couple, so I'm here on my own."

It reminded Henry of his own situation and he bit his bottom lip, flirting forgotten. "Sorry. I know how shitty that feels. I was supposed to be going skiing with my boyfriend, but I found him fucking his neighbour, so here I am instead." The shocked gasp from behind him had Henry clapping a hand over his mouth in horror. "I'm so sorry," he said quickly to the woman and two small children walking past him. When he glanced back at Dom, he found him grinning back, eyes alight with laughter.

"Well, my story isn't as colourful as yours. I'm still good friends with him. We just weren't working anymore together." Dom edged them further into the corner out of the way, but Henry was too busy trying not to get excited about the fact that Dom had said *him* to be offended.

Dom licked his lips, and Henry's eyes took on a life of their own, watching the swipe of Dom's pink tongue without his approval. He had full lips. Kissable lips.

Henry liked kissing.

Missed it since he'd broken up with Kyle.

"So I was thinking . . ." Dom said, snapping Henry's gaze back to his. "I know we've only just met and everything, but I was about to see if they've got any slots free at the spa—it's normally quite empty on changeover days—and I wondered if you fancied joining me?"

"Um . . ." Henry wasn't often lost for words, but he'd come away to be on his own for a week. To collect his thoughts and concentrate on himself for once. Not jump on the first hot guy he met. *Oh, who am I kidding? They're El's words, not mine.* "Yeah, okay. Sounds great." Not that Henry had ever been to a spa, but he figured they'd both be nearly naked, so how bad could it be?

Not to mention Dom's answering smile sent a welcome little flutter through his stomach that he hadn't felt in a while.

Ella had said to enjoy himself, after all.

With Dom doing the talking, they managed to book a slot from noon to three.

Luckily Henry had packed his towel and swimming shorts in his rucksack because he'd only remembered them at the last minute.

Once they'd paid, Henry shoved his hands in his pockets, not knowing what to do next. They had about another hour until their slot started, but he had no idea whether Dom wanted to go off and do something else on his own first.

"There's a café down near the lake. We could walk down, get a coffee, and sit outside if you want. Since we've got an hour to kill." He frowned and glanced outside where the sky had turned an ominous grey colour. "I know it's a bit chilly—"

"I don't mind the cold," Henry cut in quickly. Truth be told, he'd much rather be outside than in.

Dom gestured to the doors behind them. "Let's go then."

Dom SHIVERED as they stepped outside.

The cold a sharp contrast to the sticky heat of the dome area. "Christ, it's cold." He quickly zipped his coat up and pulled on his hat, turning to see Henry pulling on his beanie and his gloves. As sad as he was to see all that unruly dark hair disappear under his hat, it did highlight his blue eyes and sharp cheekbones.

"The lake is this way." Dom started to walk up the path with Henry falling into step beside him.

He didn't make a habit of approaching total strangers, especially not at a family-friendly holiday resort. But Henry had looked so out of place and lost, the caretaker in him couldn't help himself.

And Henry was hot too.

All angles and hair.

He'd only meant to offer a bit of friendly advice, but things had taken an unexpected yet very welcome turn. He grinned to himself as they walked. "What's your last name then, Henry? I feel we should share that before getting half-naked together."

Henry glanced at him, lips quirked. "That's not usually the way it happens."

Dom barked out a laugh. This was not what he'd expected when he'd seen Henry walk in through those doors. "I like to do things differently."

For a minute he wondered if Henry would answer, but after a slight pause he said, "My last name is West. I'm twenty-six and from Bristol." He grinned. "Thought I'd get it all out there, save you the trouble of asking."

"We'll have nothing left to talk about if you carry on like that."

"Sorry." Henry fiddled with the buttons on his coat. "New places make me a bit nervous, and when I'm nervous, I tend to talk a lot. And quickly." He shrugged. "I'll be fine once I get my bearings."

Dom looked around at the villas nestled in the forest and the fairy lights lining the road and nudged Henry's shoulder. "It's a holiday park in England. Not the Vegas Strip."

"I know it probably sounds stupid, but—"

Dom stopped him with a hand on his arm and waited until Henry looked at him. "*I'm* sorry. I didn't mean to make you feel self-conscious. It's not stupid at all." Guilt tugged at him, and Dom mentally kicked himself for being so insensitive.

That wasn't him at all.

Maybe his breakup had affected him more than he thought.

Resolved to do better and not give Henry the impression he was an arse, Dom made it his mission to point out everything on their walk down to the lake.

"There's more restaurants up ahead on the left." He gestured to where the roofs jutted out above the trees. "And there's a massive children's playground there too."

Henry's eyes widened as they passed it. "They never had anything like that when I was little."

"Same." Although Dom's *little* was a few years before Henry's.

As they reached the start of the raised walkway down to the lake area, Henry bumped his shoulder. "You never told me your last name."

"Spencer." He grinned. "I'm thirty-two and I'm from Somerset."

Henry smiled back, and Dom wondered if he was imagining the slight relaxing of Henry's shoulders. "Why did you decide to come here on your own?"

"Why did you?" Dom countered.

"I asked first."

Dom breathed in deep and let it out slowly while he figured what to say that wouldn't make him sound sad. "I've been coming here for a few years. Used to come with my family when I was younger. I like the familiarity." He found it easier coming back to somewhere he knew so well. "When Sam and I broke up, it just seemed like the natural thing to do."

"You didn't want to cancel or bring someone else?"

Dom raised both eyebrows. "I'm not that quick at replacing people."

Henry huffed. "I meant friends or family."

"Nah. I work with my brothers as it is. As much as I love both them and my job, I've no wish to holiday with them too. And my friends couldn't get the time off." He shrugged and gestured to the beautiful scenery laid out below and around them. "It's not exactly a hardship coming here. There's plenty to do, and I don't mind my own company." Which was true. He would've been quite happy going to the spa on his own, but Henry was an added bonus.

They walked further down the path until Henry drew to a halt and pointed up into the tall trees above them. "What's that up there."

Dom glanced up to see the aerial walkway course: ropes and wooden walkways of all shapes and sizes strung between the tree trunks. "It's the aerial walkway." He gestured over his shoulder. "The start of it is back there a bit. You walk up into the trees, then make your way around the course and there's a zipwire at the end."

Henry stared at him, then looked up again, frowning like he couldn't parse what Dom had said. "It doesn't look that high from down here."

Dom laughed. "Yeah, I know, but trust me, it seems a lot higher when you're up there." Not that Dom was all that bothered by heights, but the first time he'd done the walkway had been a bit of a shock, because Henry was right, it didn't look all that bad from down here. But once you were balancing on the wooden steps, swaying from side to side, it soon got a little hairy.

Especially if it was wet. But the zipwire ride at the end was awesome. "You fancy it?"

Henry visibly shuddered. "Err . . . no thanks."

They reached the bottom of the path and Dom pointed to the group of buildings up ahead. "That's the sports pavilion. They've indoor climbing, badminton, tennis, and Astroturf football pitches out the back. Lots of other smaller stuff too." Maybe Henry would want to do some of those things with him since they were both on their own? Dom didn't voice his thoughts though, one step at a time. He pointed to a couple of small buildings to the left. "And that there is where they run all the kid's crèche things."

Henry laughed. "I can hear."

He had a lovely smile. When it reached his eyes like that, it lit up his whole face, and Dom got caught staring.

"Where's this coffee you promised me?" Henry's cheeks were dusted pink, and Dom didn't know if it was from the cold or Dom's blatant appreciation.

Not wanting to make things awkward between them, Dom smiled and looked ahead to where they were going. "Just up here. Come on."

As Dom predicted, the inside part of the café and the sports bar next door were full to bursting, but the seats outside were empty apart from a few hardy customers. After collecting their drinks, Dom led them back outside and took a seat at one of the spare tables.

It was cold, but hopefully the coffee would help keep them warm for a bit.

"So," Dom began, sipping his drink and stealing a glance at Henry. He was busy admiring their surroundings, gaze darting from place to place. "You never told me how you ended up here on your own?"

"I did." Henry frowned. "I told you my skiing trip got cancelled because I caught my boyfriend fucking his neighbour."

"Oh, yes. Me and half the people at reception." Dom chuckled at Henry's groan of embarrassment. "But why did you come *here* when it's obviously not your type of place?" Dom waited while Henry seemed to struggle for an answer.

Eventually he set his mug down and rubbed at his temples as though he had a headache forming. "I got very drunk with my sister after I walked in on Kyle and his wandering penis."

Dom choked a little on his drink. "Thanks for that image."

Henry smirked. "Ella, that's my sister, knows someone who works in one of the restaurants here. Apparently they'd had a few late cancellations and he got her a friends-and-family deal. So it was, um . . . cheap." He looked down at his drink, and Dom got the impression he hadn't meant to say that bit.

"Didn't you get a refund from your skiing trip?" Surely that would've cost way more than a week at a UK holiday village, considering it wasn't school holidays or anything.

Henry bit his lip, his cheeks growing pinker by the second, and Dom was beginning to wish he'd never asked.

"You don't have to talk about this if it makes you uncomfortable. I was just curious." And that curiosity had only increased with Henry's reluctance to answer, but Dom wasn't the type to push.

Henry seemed to waver for a moment before slumping in his seat. "Kyle paid for the trip. I just saved my spending money."

"That was nice of him?" It didn't seem to fit with someone who'd then cheat. Assuming they'd been exclusive.

"In a way, I suppose it was. He really wanted to go, so I guess it was either pay for me or go on his own. But I'm scared of heights, so I'm not convinced my enjoyment featured heavily in his plans."

A surprised laugh escaped Dom. "You're afraid of heights and yet he booked a skiing trip for you?"

Henry nodded. "Yep."

"Wow."

"I know. I guess that should've been a clue that he was a bit of an arse."

Dom agreed. Anyone who ignored their partner's fears like that wasn't a keeper. But then, "I know it's none of my business, and feel free to tell me to fuck off, but why did you agree to go?"

Henry scowled and Dom braced himself, expecting to be told where to go. "You sound like my sister." His features evened out then, and he sighed. "I don't know why I went along with it, really. Maybe I felt like I had to since he'd paid and everything. I've only just finished uni, so I've not got loads of money to spare. I felt bad for never being able to do stuff, I guess."

Now it was Dom's turn to frown. "I thought you said you were twenty-six?"

"I am." Henry raised an eyebrow, as if challenging Dom to comment. "Not everyone goes to uni straight from school. I wanted to save up a bit first so I didn't have horrendous loans when I finished."

"Fair enough." They'd been talking for so long that when Dom glanced at his watch, it was almost quarter to twelve. "You ready?" He gestured to Henry's mug. "It's almost time for our slot."

Henry drained the last of his drink and stood. "Lead the way."

They walked round the lake towards the spa in silence. Not exactly awkward, but not comfortable either. Dom wondered if Henry regretted saying all that to a virtual stranger. "Look," he said, drawing Henry to a halt. "I'm sorry if I've made you uncomfortable. We've only just met, and I asked you some pretty personal questions."

Henry met his gaze. "You did. But I asked you some earlier, so fair's fair, I guess." He glanced at the lake and slipped his hands into his pockets, looking suddenly shy. "I didn't mind. For some reason, I find you easy to talk to. Maybe it's because you are a stranger and I'm never going to see you again after this. So what does it matter?"

That last part stung, but Dom hid his reaction. They *were* strangers. Why would Henry want to spend any more time with him when he'd obviously come away for some time alone? "Maybe." He carried on walking, but as he reached for the door to the spa, he turned to Henry and offered a small smile. "For what it's worth, it's easy to talk to you too."

CHAPTER 2

"*J*esus." Henry sucked in a breath as he closed the glass door behind him. Hot didn't even begin to describe it. The air felt heavy and wet, sweat already covering his skin as he sat down on one of the benches in the sauna. "Will Lucifer be joining us any time soon?"

Dom laughed. "I wouldn't say no to Tom Ellis."

"Me neither, although I'm not sure I'd be capable of anything in this heat."

"It's not that bad."

"It's roasting." So hot, in fact, Henry also struggled to appreciate the sight of a tattooed and glistening Dom in his black and grey swimming shorts. He let his head fall back against the wall behind him and tried to relax, but *fucking hell*, it was hot.

"It's good for you. Opens up all your pores, lets you sweat out the bad stuff."

Henry grunted. "Assuming I don't die of heat stroke."

According to Dom and the leaflet Henry had been handed when he walked in, there were many different rooms to try out, each one with a slightly different experience.

Admittedly, he hadn't paid all that much attention to it and had no idea what *experience* they were in at that moment, but despite the intense heat, Henry did find himself relaxing.

Dom nudged his knee against Henry's. "See, not so bad once you get used to it."

"I wouldn't go as far as to say I'm used to it." Nor was he used to the way the fleeting touch of Dom's leg had made his stomach flutter. "I think it's more that my body has accepted defeat." Sweat trickled from his hairline down the side of his face, and Henry wiped at it with the back of his hand. He chuckled to himself.

Pretty sure Dom isn't interested, considering I must look like shit right now.

He didn't need a mirror to picture his red face, sweaty unruly hair, and the lack of a six-pack. Just as Henry glanced down at his relatively flat but undefined stomach, the door to their room pushed open and a tall, blond, tanned specimen of a man in peak physical condition walked in.

Wonderful.

The man smiled, showing off equally perfect white teeth, and Henry found himself sitting up straighter and sucking his belly in. Dom's soft laughter sounded beside him, and Henry turned to see Dom staring at him, one eyebrow raised. "What?" he mouthed, shaking his head a little.

"Come on." Dom stood and held a hand out for Henry, which Henry automatically took. "I think we've been in here long enough."

He led them out into the main area, and Henry sighed in relief when the cooler air hit his skin. "That feels so nice."

Still holding his hand, Dom tugged Henry over to a couple of waterfall showers near the far wall. "Come shower off and we'll go for a swim."

Henry wasn't normally one to hold hands, at least he didn't think he was. None of the men he'd ever been with had initiated it, so neither had he. Dom's hand was big and rough, but comforting at the same time. Henry liked it and was then a little disappointed when Dom let go of him to start one of the showers.

He pointed to the wall and grinned. "It's got lots of different settings. Give them all a go."

Henry studied the instructions and went for one that sounded interesting. "Fuck me!" He hissed and jumped sideways as water thundered down on his shoulders and back like a thousand tiny fists pummelling his skin.

Dom's laughter echoed around them, and Henry glared as he hurriedly changed options on his shower to something a little less intense. "You could've warned me," he muttered before tipping his head back and letting the cool water wash the sweat from his face and hair.

"I could've. But where's the fun in that?"

Henry ignored him in favour of playing with a few more settings, none of them thankfully as bad as the first. Closing his eyes, he enjoyed the feel of the spray on his skin, wondering how he'd ended up here exactly.

Showering with a stranger.

Not that Dom felt like a stranger. He'd meant what he'd said outside, talking to Dom was easy. Henry had told him things he'd struggled to tell even his best friends.

"Hey."

Henry opened his eyes to see Dom staring at him, drops of water clinging to his lashes. He'd let his shower turn off, and Henry took a moment to appreciate the sight of a wet Dom. His blond hair, turned dark by the water, clung to his forehead, and Henry raised his hand to push it back a little when Dom's voice startled him.

"Want to try out the pool?"

Henry snatched his hand back and rubbed his neck, pretending like he hadn't been about to touch Dom at all. Nope.

"Pool?" he managed, a husky edge to his voice that he wanted to roll his eyes at.

Seriously, Henry? It's not like you've never seen a hot man before.

Dom studied him, amusement in his eyes, but he didn't call Henry out on his ogling. "There's a pool through there." He gestured behind them through a set of double doors. "Half inside, half out." He smiled, eyes crinkling at the corners. "Shall we?"

Henry's breath caught, those pesky flutters in his stomach reminding him what it was like to experience the first heady moments of attraction. "Yeah, okay." He smiled, Kyle fast becoming a distant memory while Dom stood in front of him looking like that.

The area around the small pool was virtually empty, only a lone woman relaxing on one of the sun loungers. She paid them no attention, far too busy doing a crossword.

Dom lowered himself to sit on the pool edge, stomach muscles bunching and releasing as he eased into the water. Henry licked his lips, eyes tracking the water droplets running over Dom's broad, inked shoulders as he leant his arms on the side and grinned. "Come on in."

That smile did funny things to Henry's insides, and he quickly slipped into the water before it did things to other parts of him too. Cooler than he was expecting, he gasped and turned to glare at Dom. "It's cold." At least he didn't have to worry about embar-rassing semis.

Dom rolled his eyes, but his smile remained. "It's not cold. The surrounding air is warm, that's all. Besides, it's supposed to be refreshing."

Henry huffed.

Refreshing.

Fucking freezing, more like.

Henry floated onto his back and tried to get used to the cool temperature. *I guess it's not so bad.*

Dom copied him, his hand brushing Henry's as he floated alongside him.

Not bad at all.

When he'd arrived a couple of hours ago, wary and disoriented, this was not how he'd expected his afternoon to go. His mind wandered to what might happen after they left the sauna, but he quickly stopped that train of thought.

Dom probably had plans.

Plans that didn't include Henry.

Shaking off the flare of disappointment that caused, Henry straightened in the water and turned to look where the thick plastic curtains led to the outside part of the pool. "Let's go outside." He glanced over his shoulder to find Dom watching him, and his smile was automatic. Something about Dom made him smile more today than he had in the last few weeks.

Feeling an usual mixture of giddy and unsettled, Henry decided it would be a good idea to make a race out of it and started swimming as if his life depended on it.

Unfortunately, he'd momentarily forgotten about the plastic curtain that blocked his way. His arm hit it first, bringing Henry to an abrupt halt, Dom's laughter sounding behind him.

"I did wonder what you were doing." He swam up next to Henry and pulled some of the plastic aside for Henry to swim through.

Cheeks no doubt flaming, Henry ducked under Dom's arm with a muttered "thank you" and swam into the middle of the pool. Although the sun had come out, it was still the end of November and it was chilly.

But definitely worth coming outside.

Henry trod water and surveyed the surroundings. Fairy lights clung to both real and artificial trees. Illuminated animals hid amongst the branches and Henry found himself smiling.

Again.

"It's nice, right?"

He turned to see Dom staring at the decorations with a wistful look.

"Yeah, it is, but you've seen it all before, haven't you?" Henry was almost positive Dom said he'd been at this time of year before.

"I have." Dom faced him, swimming close enough to Henry that their legs brushed under the water. Henry shivered and wasn't wholly convinced it was from the cold. "But I still love it. Christmas is one of my favourite times of the year."

Henry snorted. Of course it was.

"You're not a fan?" He looked slightly disappointed, and Henry didn't like that at all.

"It's not that I don't like it. I—" He'd been about to say *live with three blokes*, but for some reason didn't want to admit that to Dom. "—didn't tend to go overboard while at uni. I've got used to half-arsing it." The disappointed look turned into something a lot like pity, and Henry wasn't a fan of that either. "Anyway . . ." He rubbed his arms and made a show of being cold. "It's freezing out here. How about we go back in, and you show me some more of those sauna rooms?"

"So . . ." Henry rocked back on his heels, hands shoved deep into his pockets. Three o'clock had come around far quicker than he'd expected, and they'd eventually left the spa and took the long walk back to the car park to collect their cars.

Henry knew what to do next as far as his holiday was concerned: drive to his villa, unload, then take his car back to the car park where it would remain for the next week.

What he wasn't so sure of was what happened with Dom. Was this it? They'd had a nice afternoon, but was he now on his own? This was unchartered territory and Henry had no idea how to handle it.

Dom didn't appear to have that problem though. He readjusted his rucksack on his shoulder and fixed Henry with a look that pinned him in place. "What are your plans for tonight?"

"Um . . ." Henry glanced away, not sure why he was suddenly reluctant to share that ordering takeaway had been his sole plan for the evening. But Dom looked at him expectantly and Henry forced out the words. "Not much. Thought I'd order some food and relax in the villa." Wow, when he said it out loud like that, he sounded like the most boring arse ever. He was on holiday, for fuck's sake.

To his surprise, Dom smiled at him. "Same. Although I've brought a chilli with me for tonight. Just need to pick up some crusty bread."

Henry laughed, couldn't help it. "Well, aren't we a pair of exciting fuckers."

"I was going to ask if you wanted to join me." Dom took a step closer, his boot nudging Henry's. "Pretty sure we could find something to do."

Each other?

Dom was flirting, right? He wasn't imagining that, was he? Wishful thinking had got him in trouble before now. "Such as?" he heard himself ask and wanted to kick himself in the shin when Dom chuckled.

"Well . . ." He reached up and tucked a stray strand of hair back under Henry's beanie, fingers lingering a moment and Henry inhaled sharply. Even with gloves on, Dom's touch did things to him. "I was hoping I could impress you with my cooking, maybe coax you into a walk after and then . . ." He shrugged, and Henry was desperate to know what thoughts were running through Dom's mind.

And then have wild and raunchy sex?

Or *and then you fuck off back to your own villa?*

Henry sucked his bottom lip between his teeth. A habit he'd developed lately when he was thinking hard about something.

He'd known Dom for a grand total of six hours. Did he really want to get naked with him?

When Dom pulled off his glove and slowly ran his thumb over Henry's lip, rescuing it from his teeth, a shiver ran through him and the decision was easy. If Dom was offering sex, then Henry was one hundred per cent on board with that.

If that's what he was offering. And there was only one way to find out. "Yeah. I'd love to join you for some chilli."

"Great." Dom beamed at him, hand brushing the back of Henry's. "What villa are you in?"

"Um . . ." Henry fished the key out of his pocket. "192."

Dom's smile got wider, and he nodded like he knew exactly where that was. "That's not too far from the dome. It's a good location to be in. I'm 256."

"Which is where?" Henry had no idea if that was close to him or not without looking at the map. The numbering scheme made no sense.

"A bit further up the road, but not too far." He fished his keys out of his pocket. "How about I come get you in a couple of hours? That should give us time to unpack, and you can come to the shop with me on the way back to mine."

Two hours? How much stuff did Dom think he had? But Henry nodded. "Sounds good."

They parted ways after exchanging phone numbers, and Henry managed to find his car without too much trouble. He followed the signs to his villa, weaving past parked cars busy unloading what looked like a month's worth of stuff. Henry had brought a small suitcase and his rucksack.

Clearly holidaying with small children meant you had to bring half your house.

Finally, he found number 192, and parked in the small space just off the road. The villa itself was set back from the road and staggered with the villas either side of it.

Pulling his suitcase and with his rucksack over his shoulder,

Henry walked up the path to his front door and let himself in. His phone rang as the door clicked shut behind him, and he rolled his eyes when he saw his sister's name on the screen.

"I've just this second stepped inside the door. How did you know?"

Laughter met his words. "I'm just that good. And hello to you too."

"Sorry. Hello. What can I do for you?"

"Since you're already inside, you can FaceTime me and show me around."

"Fine." Henry ended the call and immediately FaceTimed Ella, flicking the camera as soon as she answered so she could see everything. "This is the living area." He panned around while she ooh'd and ahh'd. It was all open plan—making the most of the space. Not huge but bigger than Henry had been expecting. Everything looked modern, and as he walked over to the patio windows, he saw his villa overlooked a small pond in amongst the trees.

"Oh, nice view," Ella cooed. "You might get squirrels and ducks visiting you there."

Henry huffed and flipped the camera around to raise an eyebrow at her. "So I won't be sad and lonely on my own, you mean?"

She tsked at him. "No. I just meant you'll probably see a bit of wildlife while you're there." She grinned. "You'll still be sad and lonely; a few squirrels won't change that."

"Fuck off." His mind immediately went to Dom, and a smile formed without his permission.

"What's that little smile for?" Ella's eyes narrowed and then went comically wide. "Oh my god, I know that smile. But surely you can't have met someone in the few hours you've been there?"

Henry blushed and Ella's laughter filled the room.

"Only you, Henry." She shook her head, eyes dancing with amusement. "Only fucking you."

"It's not like that," he grumbled. It was totally like that.

Her raised eyebrows called bollocks. "Tell me how it is then?"

He sighed, but knew she'd never let it drop without getting all the details. And he'd be exactly the same in her position so he couldn't even be mad. "His name's Dom, and he's here on his own after splitting up with his boyfriend. He's thirty-two and lives in Somerset somewhere."

She let out a squeak, smiling widely at him. "It's fate."

Henry rolled his eyes.

"When are you seeing him again?"

"In a couple of hours. He's walking over to pick me up. Then we're going back to his villa for some chilli."

"Wow. Well done, Henry. Way to make the most of your week."

A laugh burst out of him. "He's probably just being nice as I looked so fucking pitiful when he first met me this morning."

"Meh. Even so, a pity fuck isn't the worst thing ever." She laughed again when Henry scowled and held up a hand. "Sorry, I'm sure that's not what this is."

"I'm not actually sure what it is." And that was the truth, but to be honest, he was more than happy to go over to Dom's with no idea where it might lead. Even if he just came straight back after eating, it would make a nice change from the moping around he'd been doing lately. "Anyway, I need to go, El. Got to take my car back and then have a shower before I go to Dom's."

She smirked. "Oh yes. Better make sure you're all clean for your 'chilli.'" She used air quotes.

"Bye." Henry ended her call mid-laugh.

His phone chimed with a text a second later.

Ella: Seriously though H, just go have some fun. You deserve a little no-strings hot sex. xx

Henry agreed wholeheartedly. *I do. I really fucking do.*

Henry: Thanks. Talk to you tomorrow x

Two HOURS later Henry was washed, changed, and sat on the sofa with his knee bouncing up and down. Nerves threatened to overtake him, but he forced the feeling back, checking his phone for the umpteenth time.

Even so, the knock on the door made him jump a mile, and Henry laughed at his idiocy as he got up to answer it.

He opened the door to a smiling Dom. "Hey."

"Hey." Henry returned his smile, giving him a quick once-over as he opened the door wide and gestured for Dom to come in. The thick fleece he wore hid the muscled chest Henry knew was there, but Dom's black jeans hugged his thighs like a second skin. Henry swallowed down the flare of anticipation. "I just need to grab my coat and keys."

Dom waited just inside the door while Henry slipped his coat on and picked up his keys. Two steps towards the door, Henry paused.

He had a couple of condoms and a small bottle of lube in his wash bag, because he was ever the optimist. *Should I take them for tonight? Was that where they were headed?*

It wasn't like he'd picked Dom up in a club where sex of some sort was almost a certainty. This was a holiday park and Dom had invited him round for dinner.

In his imagination, that meant a quick bite to eat, then an evening of fucking on the pristine white sheets of the huge bed the villas seemed to come with. But that was all in his head and rarely translated to real life. They hadn't even so much as kissed. Maybe he wasn't Dom's type?

In reality, Henry was adrift in uncharted waters without a clue how to navigate. "Um . . ." He shifted from foot to foot, unsure how to broach the subject without sounding both presumptuous and possibly a bit of an arse. "Do I need to bring anything?"

"Such as?"

Heat crept up Henry's neck and he could well imagine the faint blush colouring his skin. He watched, mortified, as Dom's gaze dropped to his throat and slowly crept back up, understanding seeming to dawn on him.

Dom grinned. "I think I'm prepared for every eventuality."

"Awesome." It came out more of a squeak than a word and Henry died a little inside.

Fuck's sake. Could you be any more awkward?

The likelihood of anything sex-related happening between them would be nil at this rate. They hadn't even made it outside and he'd already made a twat of himself.

The sigh that slipped out was heavier than he'd intended, and Dom's gaze shot to his.

"Are you okay?" He took a step closer until they were only inches apart. "If you'd rather not come to mine for dinner tonight, that's totally fine, Henry. I'm not going to force you." He smiled, warm and inviting, soothing the nerves threatening to ruin Henry's evening before it had begun.

"I'm fine, and I do want to spend the evening with you. It's just . . ." He bit his lip, wondering how honest to be with someone he'd only met that morning.

"Just what?" Dom waited for him to answer, hands tucked into his pockets, an air of patience surrounding him like he'd give Henry all the time in the world to answer.

And it was that easy manner that tipped Henry over the edge. Dom gave the impression that simple honesty would be more welcome than any bullshit, no matter how blunt that truth might be.

Henry took a deep breath and let it all spill out. "I don't know what this is?" He quickly gestured between the two of them. "Are we just having a friendly dinner and that's it? Or will there be sex after? I know that's a big assumption on my part because you might not fancy me at all. It's not like we're hooking up in a club or anything." His eyes widened and Henry knew he was starting to ramble, but the words didn't want to stop despite his brain trying valiantly to rein them in. "I mean, it's not like we've even kissed, so—"

Dom gently cupped Henry's jaw, his palms rough against his skin as he tilted his chin up to meet his gaze. "Yes, I'm inviting you round for a friendly dinner, because I like you. We're both on our own, and I thought why the fuck not."

"Okay." Disappointing but not the end of the world.

I can do friends.

Dom didn't move his hands, though. Instead, he stroked a thumb ever so softly over Henry's cheekbone. The light touch making him shiver. "To answer your other questions, I absolutely do fancy you, but I have no expectations for anything this evening. Just that we eat and have a good time. And if that turns out to include sex of some sort, then yes, I have the necessities."

"Good to know." Henry smiled, couldn't help it. He also couldn't help the way his gaze drifted to Dom's mouth. He was so close, if Henry moved an inch or two forward . . .

"And as for not even kissing yet . . ." Dom raised an eyebrow in question, and Henry took that for the invitation it was and closed the remaining distance between them, slipping his arms around Dom's waist.

His lips were cold against Henry's, soft though, and his heart swooped. This was the first kiss he'd experienced since Kyle, and it was far easier than he'd expected to lose himself to the touch of another man. Dom made no move to deepen it, and Henry was fine with that. Being close to him like this was more than enough for now. He closed his eyes, the subtle scent of Dom's aftershave teasing his senses, and he lingered for a moment longer before pulling back. They still had to go shopping after this, and Henry had no wish to wander up and down the grocery aisles with an erection.

It took a lot of willpower to step back and put a little distance between them when every part of Henry wanted to explore Dom's mouth and turn their kiss into something far more X-rated.

"So now that we've got all that out of the way," Dom said, reaching for Henry's hand and twining their fingers. "Shall we go do a bit of shopping and then head back to mine?" He met Henry's gaze, the heat in his eyes igniting a spark inside Henry that would take very little encouragement to turn into a roaring flame.

"Yeah. Okay." He swallowed and stepped outside, tugging Dom after him. Hopefully the cold night air would have the same effect as a cold shower. Locking the door after Dom, Henry let him lead the way back towards the main domed area.

Night had well and truly settled in, and Henry glanced up at the lights illuminating their path every few feet. The road was eerily quiet and he was struck by how weird it was not to see any cars. "It's quite nice having to walk everywhere."

"Yeah." Dom squeezed his hand and Henry hid his smile, glancing instead at the villas on his side of the road. "It's one of the things I really like about it. Lots of fresh air and no road rage."

Henry snorted. Dom seemed like the last person to get road rage. "I bet you stick to the speed limit all the time."

Dom turned to him, eyebrow raised. "I do, as a matter of fact. They're in place for a reason. That doesn't stop me getting pissed off with idiots who seem to think they can set their own speed limits and fuck the consequences." He let go of Henry's hand to run his fingers through his hair. "Sorry."

Henry frowned. "What for?"

"I didn't mean to get all preachy about it." He had a funny expression and it suddenly dawned on Henry that Dom thought he might have offended him. That maybe Henry was one of *those* drivers.

The idea of it made him laugh out loud.

Which, of course, Dom took totally the wrong way. His back stiffened, expression morphing into a scowl. "Dangerous driving isn't a laughing matter."

Henry's laughter cut off abruptly and he quickly moved in front of Dom, stopping him walking with a hand on his arm. "That wasn't why I was laughing, honestly. I totally agree with you."

Dom's eyebrows scrunched in confusion. "Then why laugh?"

"Because I know you were thinking that I was probably some reckless arsehole that ignores all speed limits." Henry gave him a pointed look and Dom winced.

"I might have considered it."

"I know. And the reason I was laughing is that I *do* drive like a grandma. Well, not my grandma because she's a nightmare and shouldn't really be on the roads, but that's beside the point. I got caught speeding once, had to go to the speed school thing and that's four hours I never ever want to repeat. And some of the stuff they cover really got to me." He shrugged. It had been the most uncomfortable afternoon he'd ever experienced. "So now I stick to the limits religiously."

"Oh." Dom took his hand again, much to Henry's delight, fingers twined loosely together. "Sorry for misjudging you." He smiled, eyes full of warmth, stirring something in Henry he refused to acknowledge.

He swallowed, looking down at their joined hands. "It's fine. No offence taken. It's not like you know me or anything."

"Yet," Dom murmured.

"What?" Henry glanced up, getting caught once again in Dom's gaze.

"It's not like I know you well, *yet*." Without elaborating further, he started walking again, tugging Henry along with him. "Come on. I can't remember what time the shop shuts, and I don't want to get there too late."

He held Henry's hand all the way there. Being at the holiday park, away from his everyday life, seemed to give everything a slightly unreal quality. He doubted very much he'd be strolling hand in hand down the road with a bloke he'd just met if he was anywhere else.

It didn't feel wrong or awkward though, so Henry decided to take it at face value and just enjoy the moment.

CHAPTER 3

Heat hit them like a wall as the doors swished open and Dom let go of Henry's hand to quickly unzip his coat. Holding it in the first place had seemed like the natural thing to do, maybe habit leftover from being with Sam. Who knew? But Henry hadn't seemed to mind, so Dom had thought, what the hell? Being tactile was something he enjoyed. Not everyone felt that way, but having Henry's fingers wrap around his was . . . nice. He hadn't realised how much he'd missed simple things like that until now.

The park shop was relatively empty, so it didn't take long to get what he needed. When he picked up a packet of rice, Henry laughed beside him.

"And here I was thinking you were all super organised." His eyes danced with laughter. "Fancy bringing chilli but no rice."

Dom rolled his eyes. "I must have forgot to pack it." Setting it in his trolley, he nudged Henry with his shoulder. "At least I'm not the one with a totally empty fridge." He shot a pointed look at the items Henry had added. Tea bags, milk, bread, and a few more essentials. "Did you expect it to come fully stocked?"

"No, I—" Henry broke off with a shrug. "To be honest, I was trying not to think about coming here at all."

Dom came to a stop in the middle of the aisle. "If you weren't looking forward to it, why bother coming at all?" Coming here on his own had felt bittersweet for Dom in some ways, but he'd still wanted to come. Still looked forward to a week away, relaxing and being outdoors.

Henry sighed, his shoulders sagging like he had the weight of the world on them. "I know it makes me an ungrateful arse. Not everyone gets to come somewhere as lovely as this for a holiday. I was just . . ." He blew out another breath and gave Dom a sheepish look. "I was wallowing in self-pity and wanted to hate everything."

A laugh burst out of him, and Dom quickly held a hand up to apologise. "Sorry, don't know where that came from. You have every right to be upset still."

Henry reached for the trolley and started pushing it, so Dom walked beside him. "I don't know why it affected me so much. We weren't together all that long, and deep down I knew he was a bit of a wanker. It's just . . ." He shrugged again, looking a little bit lost, and Dom couldn't help himself.

"Hey." He glanced around to check they were alone, then cupped Henry's jaw, gently urging him to meet his eyes. "We feel how we feel. It doesn't matter if you were together six months or six years. What happened hurt you and you're allowed to feel how you like about that. So what if you thought you were going to hate it here. You came anyway, and I'm hoping it's not as bad as you were expecting."

Henry stared at him, and for whatever reason, Dom held his breath waiting for his reply.

A slow smile crept over Henry's face, and he placed a hand over Dom's. "It's not been too bad so far."

Dom laughed, the sound loud in the quiet of the shop. "Well, let's see if we can't improve on *not too bad.*"

He steered them to the checkout, shaking his head, with Henry's wide smile burnt into memory.

Once outside, Dom led Henry up the pathway instead of the steps. "Let's go this way. I want to show you the outside pool."

Henry zipped up his coat and then took his bag of food from Dom to carry. "Didn't we come this way earlier?"

"Yes, but it's so much better at night." Well, in Dom's opinion it was. But then he was a sucker for all things Christmassy. As they walked up to the small viewing platform, he reached for Henry's hand again, smiling at his small gasp of surprise.

"Wow. They really do go all out, don't they?" He stared out at the illuminated trees that surrounded the outdoor pool area, bathing it in warm, magical light. A winter wonderland to swim amongst under the stars. "Is that like a lazy river? I didn't really pay that much attention earlier."

"Kind of. You don't get floats. The water's faster and you kind of half swim, half get swept along. Seems faster at night too." He turned away from the water to face Henry. "We should come swimming at night. It's a lot less busy and not too many kids."

Neither of them had mentioned meeting up beyond tonight, but Dom was a big believer in putting himself out there. The worst Henry could do was say no. And if he did, then fair enough.

Henry stared back at the water, watching a couple of teenage boys laugh as they slid face first down one of the long wide slides. "Aren't we a bit old for that?" He gestured with the hand holding his shopping bag.

Dom scoffed. "No. It's fun. Since when are you too old to have a bit of fun?" As he said it, a group of adults came around the corner in a tangle of limbs, their loud laughter drifting up to where Dom and Henry stood. "See?" He bumped Henry's shoulder. "Fun." They watched as the group raced down the slide then proceeded to get stuck in the whirlpool at the bottom, their laughter only getting louder. "No one cares how old you are, Henry."

Dom watched him out of the corner of his eye, saw the moment he seemed to accept Dom's words.

"Yeah," he said after a moment. "We could do that."

Dom didn't push for a day or time, better to see how their night went first. But the fact that Henry was open to spending more time with him left him with a smile that lasted all the way back to his villa.

"Just put your whole bag in the fridge. There should be room." Dom said as he let them inside. "That way you won't forget anything later." He set his own bag on the worktop and started to unpack his shopping.

Henry opened the fridge door and whistled. "How long are you planning on staying?" Glancing back at Dom, he gestured to the well-stocked shelves.

"A week. Same as you." Dom didn't add that although he didn't mind being here on his own, he hadn't fancied eating out with no one to talk to or share it with. Not this time around anyway.

"You're not gonna starve, are you?" After squashing his things in alongside Dom's, Henry stood. "Can I help with anything?"

Dom had already put the rice on to boil and the chilli to heat through. "You can get us a couple of beers, if you fancy one?"

"Yeah, I'd love one." He fetched two Desperados out of the fridge, opened them, then looked at Dom expectantly. "Limes?"

"In the fruit bowl." Dom pointed to the full bowl on the counter and picked a lime from the top. "Here." He sliced a couple of segments and passed them to Henry, who then popped one in each bottle. "Cheers." He handed one to Dom and they clinked bottles.

Dom took a long pull, enjoying the sharp taste of the lime alongside the lager. The evening so far had moved along nicely, spending time with Henry almost natural in its easiness. But now they were back at Dom's villa waiting for dinner to cook, tension crept into the air between them. No, maybe tension wasn't the right word.

Anticipation.

That was probably a better descriptor.

It surrounded them, almost tangible as they stood, beers in hand, looking at each other. Silence stretched between them for so long that Dom chuckled. "I feel like one of us needs to make a move to get the awkwardness out of the way."

Henry's shoulders sagged and he set his beer on the worktop. "Thank god. I thought it was me imagining things. But it got weird, right?"

Dom nodded. "Maybe a little."

"I was all right at the shop and on the walk here. But now that everything's done and we're here . . . waiting . . ." He huffed out a laugh and rubbed the back of his neck. "I don't know what to do now."

"We don't have to do anything." Dom didn't want Henry to feel pressured or anything.

"I know we don't." Henry took a step towards him and stopped, leaving a few inches between them. "But I really fucking want to."

"Me too." Dom set his beer down and stepped into Henry's space, wrapping his arms around his waist and pulling him close enough to kiss. As their lips met for the second time that day, Henry's arms wound around his neck, and Dom moaned.

If someone had told him that he'd spend his first night on holiday kissing a bloke in his villa, he'd have laughed and called them ridiculous. This was so not the place to pick up men. It had been the furthest thing from his mind.

But now that he had the solid weight of Henry pressed against him, the scrape of stubble on his skin as they kissed, he realised it was exactly what he needed. Yes, it still felt a little weird to be kissing someone other than Sam, but they'd been over for a while now, and having Henry in his arms was refreshing in a way he struggled to put into words. He was about as far away from Sam as you could get, and maybe that was why Dom had fallen into this so easily.

He slipped a hand under the back of Henry's T-shirt, fingers brushing warm skin, and pulled him closer. The nudge of his hardening cock alongside Dom's sent a lick of heat up his spine. Fuck the chilli, he wanted Henry naked, wanted to see him as well as feel.

Pulling back enough to meet his gaze, Dom smiled. "I reckon I could eat later. What about you?"

Henry licked across his bottom lip, a slow grin forming. "Yeah, I'm not that hungry all of a sudden."

Reaching behind him, Dom turned off both the rice and the chilli, then took Henry's hand. As nice as the sofa was in the villa, it wasn't up to two six-foot blokes messing around on it. Not if they wanted to avoid injury.

"Bedroom?" he asked, because while he was pretty certain they were on the same wavelength, Dom wanted to be sure.

Henry's eyes darkened as he swept his gaze over Dom, lingering over the growing bulge in his jeans. Dom adjusted himself, taking his time, and Henry swallowed. "Yeah," he said, voice rough enough to make Dom's heart race. "Lead the way."

The bedside light cast a warm glow over the room as Dom led Henry through the door. Crisp, white sheets covered the king-sized bed, and Dom sat down on the edge, positioning Henry between his legs.

He ran his hands up the back of Henry's thighs, the strong lean muscle firm under his fingertips. Looking up, he captured Henry's gaze and slowly traced the seam of his jeans up over his arse and back down again.

Henry's sharp inhale, loud in the silence, lit a flame inside him and Dom moved his hands up and round Henry's waistband, until they rested on the button of his jeans.

He waited a moment, enjoying the quick rise and fall of Henry's chest as his breaths came quicker. His own heart raced, anticipation gripping him tight, making it almost impossible to keep his hands still. "This okay?" he asked softly. At Henry's quick nod, Dom popped the button undone and teasingly, slowly unzipped Henry's jeans.

Dark-grey boxer briefs did little to hide the bulge inside them, and Dom traced his thumb over the head of Henry's cock, smiling at the wet patch already there. He gripped the shaft when Henry pushed his hips forward and glanced up to find Henry watching him, cheeks flushed, pupils blown, and bottom lip caught between his teeth again. His hair was mussed, like he'd had his hands in it, and Dom didn't think he'd seen anything hotter in a long, long while.

Leaning in, he pressed his face to Henry's groin, breathing in the heady scent of sex, his hands still holding Henry through the material of his underwear.

"Fuck," Henry murmured, hands coming to rest on Dom's shoulders. "I want you to—"

He broke off so suddenly, Dom sat back and looked up at him. "Want me to what?"

Hooking his finger in the waistband of Henry's jeans and underwear, Dom eased them down enough for Henry's cock to spring free. "Suck you?"

Henry nodded. "I didn't want to sound pushy."

Dom laughed. He hadn't expected Henry to be so . . . *polite*. It was nice. Refreshing. He wrapped a hand around his length and started a long, lazy stroke. With his gaze locked on Henry's, Dom leant forward and licked the head of his cock, Henry's gasp going straight to his groin.

He tongued the slit, tasting the salty bitterness of precome before taking Henry in as far as he could.

"Fuck." Henry jerked, fingers digging into the tops of Dom's shoulders, breaths coming short and fast.

Dom smiled, lips stretched wide, and slowly backed off until just the head was in his mouth. He lingered, paying attention to all the spots that he found sensitive, and judging by Henry's soft moans of pleasure, they had the same effect on him.

With a hand curled round Henry's thigh and the other holding the base of his cock, Dom sucked him, easing him in and out of his mouth in a rhythm that had Henry swearing under his breath.

Still in his jeans and underwear, Dom shifted on the edge of the bed, his erection pressing against the zip. He reached a hand down, fumbling with the button, unable to quite coordinate things.

Henry's soft chuckle sounded above him moments before he stepped back and slipped out of Dom's mouth. His hand cupped Dom's chin, tilting his head up. "Clothes off, and get in bed."

Eyebrow raised, Dom said, "I thought you didn't want to sound pushy."

"This isn't pushy." Henry's eyes, dark and heavy lidded, flicked down to where his cock jutted out, wet and hard. "This is me being desperate to get you naked."

"Okay then." With nothing to distract him now, Dom made short work of undressing, clothes falling in a heap on the bedroom floor. When he glanced back up, Henry was as gloriously naked as him, and Dom couldn't help but stop to drink in the sight.

Shuffling further back on the bed he let his thighs fall open and beckoned Henry to join him. "Come here."

Henry climbed on top of him, settled in the gap Dom had made and let out a hum of pleasure as his cock brushed against Dom's. "Not how I pictured spending my first night here."

Dom laughed, though it quickly turned into a low groan, the movement increasing the friction between them. "This is better though, right?"

"Oh yeah," Henry murmured as he leant in for a kiss. Soft lips met Dom's and he opened his mouth, inviting Henry in, moaning at the sweep of his tongue against his own. Slipping a hand between them, Dom wrapped his fingers around them both, precome easing the way enough for him to glide his hand up and down their lengths.

Henry rutted against him, chasing his release, and Dom felt the tell-tale tingle of his own starting in his balls. The room filled with the sound of soft gasps and breathy moans, the quiet creak of the bed an accompaniment that increased in pace along with Dom's hand.

Henry tensed against him. "Close," he muttered, his cock stiffening moments before he came, wetness coating Dom's hand and stomach. His head dropped to Dom's shoulder, hot breath tickling his ear for a moment or two while he caught his breath.

Dom shifted slightly, painfully hard still, but his hand trapped in place by Henry's weight. He felt Henry smile against his skin. "Sorry. Let me just . . ." He settled himself beside Dom, propped up on one elbow, and reached for his cock.

Dom sucked in a breath, heart rate galloping once again with someone else's hand on him. Using some of his come as lube, Henry brought him to the edge in seconds, each sure stroke of his hand sending spikes of pleasure up his spine until Dom's toes curled, hands fisted in the sheet, and he came harder than he had in a long while.

Not surprising since he'd only had himself for company recently.

"Fuck." Running a hand through his sweat-damp hair, Dom turned to face a very smug-looking Henry. "Oh shut up." He gave a half-hearted swipe at his chest. "Like you didn't just have this exact look a few minutes ago."

Henry grinned. "Doesn't mean I can't bask in the afterglow of a job well done."

Dom barked out a laugh. How was this so easy between them? He'd expected things to be at least a little awkward post-sex;

they'd only met that morning for fuck's sake. It might seem like an age ago since he'd spied Henry, all lost and bewildered in the middle of changeover day chaos, but the reality was they were still virtually strangers.

Yet lying here together, Dom felt comfortable in a way it usually took several dates to accomplish. Deciding not to examine that too closely, he reached for Henry's hand, come-covered fingers and all. "I don't know about you, but I'm starving after that."

Henry's stomach rumbled in agreement, and he patted it with a sheepish smile. "Same."

"You fancy that chilli now?" Dom asked. A look of surprise crossed Henry's face and Dom rolled his eyes. "What, you thought I was going to kick you out? Really?"

"Well, no, but . . ." He shrugged. "I've not exactly done anything like this before. I'm not sure of the rules."

Dom was no expert either, but he did know one thing. "Why do there have to be rules? We've just had great sex and now we're hungry. There's food out there." He gestured over his shoulder towards the kitchen. "So let's clean up and go eat it."

Henry studied him for a long moment, then shrugged again, his smile small this time but intimate in a way that Dom felt deep in his chest. "Okay then."

Dressed in boxers and T-shirts, they sat at Dom's table and ate their weight in chilli, rice, and sourdough bread from the shop.

With plates wiped clean with the remaining bread, Henry sat back in his chair and groaned. "That was so good. Thank you."

"You're welcome."

Patting his belly, Henry frowned down at it. "I'm so full, you might have to roll me home." With his hair messy from earlier and a satisfied sleepy look on his face, Henry was the picture of contentment, and Dom knew in that moment that he didn't want Henry to go back to his own villa.

"You could stay."

Henry's hand stilled on his belly, and he glanced up sharply. "With you?"

"Well, there's nobody else here."

"I know that," he said carefully. "I meant, with you in your bed?" He met Dom's gaze, and Dom struggled to read his expression. Hesitance, maybe hopefulness?

"Yes, with me. In my bed." Strangers or not, the idea of sleeping with Henry all night, with maybe a repeat performance in the morning, was all kinds of appealing. Why wouldn't it be?

Henry stared back at him, mouth opening, then closing.

"If you'd rather go home, then I totally understand." Dom followed it up with a smile of his own to show that he meant it. Just because he wanted to spend the night together didn't mean Henry felt the same. And that was okay, too.

After a too-long beat of silence, when Dom had just about convinced himself that Henry was about to say no, that soft smile returned. "Yeah. I'd love to stay." Then he frowned. "I don't have anything with me though."

Now he'd agreed to stay the night, no way was Dom letting a little thing like night-time necessities get in the way of it. "You can borrow my stuff to shower with. And if you want something to sleep in, I'm sure I can find something to fit you."

He ran his tongue over his teeth and grimaced. "What about a toothbrush?"

Got that covered too.

"I brought my electric one and a pack of new heads. You can use one of those."

He raised an eyebrow. "You seem to have thought of everything."

"I just really want you to stay the night."

"Okay."

"Yeah?"

Henry grinned this time, maybe at the hopefulness Dom

knew was written all over his face. "Yeah. I don't really want to go back to my empty villa when I could be here with you."

His words made Dom's heart stutter and his belly swoop.

Stop it, he chided. *It's one night together. A bit of company for us both, nothing more.*

After clearing away their mess from dinner, they settled on the sofa. Dom turned on the TV, more for background noise than anything else. The brochure for all the park activities sat on the coffee table in front of them and Henry reached for it, smoothing his hand over the front cover.

"I suppose you've done nearly everything in here at some point, huh?"

Dom shrugged. "I've done a lot of them, but roller skating is not for me."

Henry laughed and flicked through to the picture of kids in roller skates going round a makeshift rink. "Oh I think you'd fit right in."

"Mhmm." Dom nudged his shoulder and skimmed through the pages until he came to the aerial walkway. "This is more my sort of thing." He pointed to the other tree-high activities and tapped the picture. "Or this."

Henry shuddered, then peered closer at the photo. "They let kids do it?"

Dom chuckled. "Yeah. You have to be eight, I think. Under twelves need to go with an adult."

"Oh, awesome," Henry grumbled under his breath. "Even fucking eight-year-olds can do it."

"Hey." Dom reached for his hand without a second thought, running his thumb gently over the back of Henry's knuckles. "It might not be a big deal to some people, but if you're frightened of heights, then being up there *is* a big deal. Huge. It's nothing to be ashamed of. You can't help it."

"Kyle didn't seem to see it that way." Henry stared down at

their joined hands, colour high in his cheeks, and Dom didn't think it had anything to do with him this time.

"Kyle was a bit of a cunt then, wasn't he?"

Bracing for Henry to maybe take offence at that, Dom was surprised when Henry glanced up, a wide smile lighting up his face. "He really was. I don't know why it took seeing him dick-deep in his next-door neighbour for me to realise that."

Dom didn't know whether to laugh or commiserate. He went with asking something that'd sat at the back of his mind until then. "You don't want to get back with him then?"

Henry wrinkled his nose. "Er . . . no. Not a fucking chance."

For reasons Dom didn't care to examine, that answer made him smile and settled something inside him.

He's not mine, I don't get to keep him.

And did he even want to? They'd spent the day together, that was all. Not declared their undying love for each other. *Get a fucking grip.*

A sudden yawn took him by surprise, and Dom slapped a hand over his mouth, manners kicking in.

"Am I boring you?" Henry asked just as he followed suit, his yawn cracking his jaw.

Dom smirked, eyebrow raised. "Am *I* boring *you*?"

"Sorry." Henry's smile was sheepish. "It's all this fresh air. I'm not normally this knackered by—" He checked his phone. "—nine forty-five."

Was that all it was?

It felt a lot later.

Dom suspected it was more likely the sex that had made him sleepy, since it'd been a while since he'd been with anyone. "We can go to bed if you want?"

As soon as the words left his mouth, the air seemed to grow heavier, tension seeping into the space between them. He still had a hold of Henry's hand, and Henry squeezed his fingers.

"Yeah, let's do that." He yawned again, and Dom chuckled. "Fuck, sorry. I don't know what's wrong with me." He stood and tugged on Dom's hand. "Come on, let's go to bed." His eyes were full of heat, promising more of what they'd done earlier, but they also held a weariness that made Dom want to tuck him up under the quilt.

"You go clean your teeth and whatever, I'm just going to check the doors are locked.

"Okay." Henry pulled him close before Dom had chance to move away and kissed him. Soft lips and stubble were the best combination, and Dom closed his eyes, melting against him, losing himself in the heady warmth of Henry's mouth. "Don't take too long," Henry murmured, then stepped back and dropped Dom's hand before heading into the bedroom.

The door of the en suite closing jarred Dom to his senses, and he shook his head. Henry's kisses were something else. Maybe he wasn't too tired for round two.

He checked and locked the front door, turned off the TV, and made sure the patio doors were locked. Henry was in bed waiting for him when Dom took his turn in the bathroom, but by the time he came out, his eyes were closed, and they didn't open when Dom turned out the light and got in bed beside him.

Not that Dom was all that surprised, but that kiss had stirred his cock into a semi and got his hopes up. Deciding he probably shouldn't spoon Henry without asking if he minded first, Dom turned over and settled into his pillow.

Sleep came surprisingly easy, and just as he was dropping off, Dom smiled into the covers as Henry rolled over and snuggled up behind him.

So you are a cuddler.

Dom's last thought as sleep took him was that he hoped that Henry would still be there when he woke up.

CHAPTER 4

Henry woke with hair in his face and his body pressed up against solid warmth. It took him a moment to remember the events from the previous evening that had led to this.

Ah, Dom.

Light crept through the gap in the curtains signalling it was morning, but the covers were thick and heavy, cocooning them in a wonderful heat, and Henry had no desire to leave them anytime soon.

If this had been a one-nighter back home, he'd have been out the door as soon as his eyes opened. In fact, he probably wouldn't have stayed over in the first place. But this felt different. Was it because they were on holiday? Maybe.

Whatever it was, Henry didn't have the burning urge to escape back to his villa. And if the way Dom shuffled back into him, pressing his arse against Henry's morning wood, was anything to go by, then Dom didn't want to kick him out anytime soon.

Henry had his arm around Dom's waist, hand resting on his toned stomach, and when Dom held his hand, he smiled. "Morning."

"Morning," Dom replied, voice scratchy with sleep. "I wasn't sure you'd still be here when I woke up."

"Did you want me to be?" Henry held his breath. He didn't think he'd read this wrong, but . . .

Dom pulled his arm tighter around him and moaned when Henry's cock nestled between his arse cheeks. "Yeah."

Henry smiled, warmth radiating through him from more than just the heat of the quilt. He slipped his hand from under Dom's and slid it down further until he met the unmistakable hardness of Dom's cock straining against the material of his pyjamas.

Gripping the length of him, Henry gave it a squeeze, making Dom's breath catch. "You're wide awake, then."

Dom laughed. "Yep."

Henry ground against his backside, his own erection making itself known. "Me too."

"So I see."

He kissed the back of Dom's neck, eliciting a shiver, then made his way up to just behind his ear. "What shall we do about that?"

Henry was up for anything.

Maybe not fucking, though. It was still early, and he wasn't sure he could be arsed with all that exertion first thing. Sleepy frotting, on the other hand, sounded about perfect.

Slipping his hand under the waistband of Dom's pyjamas, he gripped his cock again, skin to skin, stroking him while grinding against him from behind. "We could do this?" he suggested, kissing along Dom's neck again. "If you want?"

"Yeah," Dom breathed, arching into Henry's hand, then pushing back against him. "This's good."

They stayed like that for a moment before Henry got frustrated with the layers of clothes between him and Dom's arse.

"Can I pull these down a bit?" he asked, desperate to feel Dom's skin against his.

Dom took a second to answer, like he had to concentrate on thinking. Henry grinned.

"Hang on." Dom leant over the side of the bed before reappearing with a familiar tube in hand.

Oh yeah. This was going to be so much better.

Dom passed it to Henry, then tugged off his pyjama bottoms and kicked them onto the floor before burrowing back under the covers.

Wasting no time, Henry poured lube into his hand and coated his cock, biting his lip as he stroked himself a couple of times.

"Hey," Dom whispered, amusement in his tone. "Remember me?"

"Sorry," Henry murmured, grinning as he poured out more lube and then took hold of Dom again. "Got carried away." He started to jack Dom, slow and steady, and shuffled forward to slot his cock between Dom's arse cheeks, the slide easy now.

"Hmm . . ." Henry closed his eyes, sensation building as he thrust into the tight space. It rolled through him, picking up pace until he fell the tell-tale tingle at the base of his spine. "Close," he murmured, kissing Dom's neck.

"Yeah." Dom put his hand over Henry's, urging him to go faster, hold tighter. The room filled with the sound of soft moans and snatched breaths until finally they tumbled over the edge together.

Henry rested his forehead against the back of Dom's neck, basking in the afterglow. When he glanced down and saw the sticky mess he'd made of Dom's lower back, he chuckled. "Let me go get some tissue before we trash the sheets."

"Hurry," Dom said, holding his hand away from the duvet. "I have a fistful that's desperate to escape." He grimaced and Henry laughed even more.

He headed into the en suite and return with a wad of loo roll. After giving half to Dom, he knelt on the bed and cleaned the come from Dom's back before tossing the tissue into the nearby bin. "No one ever mentions how messy sex is."

Dom rolled onto his back after disposing of his own tissues. He met Henry's gaze, smile in place. "Worth it, though."

"Oh yeah." Henry couldn't resist leaning in for a kiss. "I'm not disputing that." He yawned and stretched his arms above his head, moaning at the satisfying crack. "What time is it anyway?" His phone was . . . somewhere. On the floor probably, lost in his pile of clothes.

Dom rolled over to the side and picked his phone up from the bedside table. "Nine fifteen." He raised an eyebrow. "Got somewhere to be?"

Henry smiled and settled back on the pillows, arms behind his head. "Nope. For once I have absolutely nowhere I need to be." It belatedly occurred to him that Dom probably did. He most likely had all sorts of plans that didn't involve lazing around in bed with the rando he'd picked up the day before. Feeling suddenly out of place and self-conscious, Henry sat up quickly. "Sorry, I bet you have things to do. I'll get dressed and be out—"

"Henry." Dom's hand on his arm stopped the flood of words and Henry let himself be tugged backwards. "You don't have to rush off."

Turning to face him, Henry sighed and pinched the bridge of his nose. *I guess it was bound to get awkward at some point.* "I bet you have plans for today, right?"

Dom nodded. "I do. I have something planned for every day that I'm here. I like to make the most of my stay."

"Such as?" Henry knew that was possibly a cue for him to make his excuses, but curiosity got the better of him. And besides, Dom had said he didn't have to rush off.

"Well . . ." Dom sat up a little and propped himself up on his elbow. "I like to start the day with a nice walk down by the lake." He pointed to the sliver of sunlight and blue sky peeking through the curtains. "Especially on a day like today."

"Fair enough," Henry conceded. Though a little chilly, a walk on such a cool, crisp morning sounded lovely. "What else?"

Dom grinned at him. "I might book the aerial walkway for Friday afternoon."

Henry shuddered, and Dom laughed. "Moving on."

"Well, there's also plenty of restaurants to check out, and there's the pool. I like to get my money's worth since its one of the only things here that's free."

"Good point."

Dom shrugged. "I fancy a massage at some point and maybe another visit to the sauna."

"Now that's more like it." That sounded far more appealing than swaying on wooden platforms in the trees.

"I had planned on playing some badminton and tennis, maybe a few games of pool. But . . ." He shrugged again, and Henry finished off the sentence in his head.

But now I'm here on my own.

Dom pursed his lips, staring at Henry for a beat too long, before taking a deep breath. And although Henry had a fair idea of what he was going to say next, the words still took him by surprise. "Maybe I could still do them, if you wanted to join me?" When Henry didn't answer immediately, he added, "Unless you've already got your own plans for the week, of course."

"I've got no plans." Henry smiled sheepishly, knowing how ridiculous that sounded. "Who comes to a place like this and has no idea of what to do, right?" He was surprised Dom wasn't rolling his eyes already.

"Plenty of people," Dom said, surprising him. "You can just chill for the week if that's what you want." He raised his hands. "No judgement here."

Henry blew out a breath and covered his eyes with his hands for a moment, needing the break because Dom's gaze was intense. And although he sensed Dom was being sincere, Henry did feel judged. "Kyle would've had an itinerary for every part of the fucking day," he mumbled, not realising he'd said it out loud until Dom reached for his hands and gently prised them away from his face.

"I thought we'd already established that Kyle was an arsehole. Hmm?" He raised his eyebrows and Henry smiled. "That's better. And if you want to spend the week doing fuck all, then do exactly that. It's entirely up to you." Twining his fingers with Henry's, he matched Henry's smile with one of his own. "But if you fancied doing a few of the things I suggested, then I would love to have some company." Giving Henry's hand a squeeze, he sat up. "Think about it while I go have a shower and then I'll make us some brekkie."

He got up and disappeared into the bathroom. Henry was half tempted to follow him, the thought of a naked and wet Dom stirring his cock to life. But instead he lay there, staring up at the ceiling wondering how things had turned so heavy.

He and Kyle had only been together for a little over six months, but clearly he'd had more of an effect on Henry than he'd realised.

Why did I let him dictate so much of our relationship?

Kyle wasn't a terrible person. Yes, he'd been a knob at the end, but he wasn't abusive. Henry had been quite happy to go along with his suggestions. Like the skiing holiday. He should've said no from the start, but he hadn't. Just like he hadn't said anything when Kyle took the piss out of him for working at Tesco.

It might not have been his dream job, but there was nothing wrong with it and it paid his bills. He'd kind of got stuck in a rut, tired of looking for a forever job he really wanted and not finding anything. And that had apparently trickled over into his personal life.

Did I think I didn't deserve better? Or was I just too apathetic to look for someone else?

Henry wasn't keen on either of those options. "Fuck me, Henry. Get a grip." He was on holiday. Had just spent the night with a hot, funny, interesting man and here he was brooding about the last six months.

That was the past.

And if it had taught him anything, it was to take the opportunities that presented themselves. Even if a small part of him thought he must be reading things wrong. On paper, Dom was way out of his league: hot, smart, had a job he said he loved.

But from the little time they'd spent together, Henry didn't peg him as a liar. If he said he wanted to spend time with Henry, then he had to believe he meant it.

And he was just so very easy to talk to that Henry had found himself doing exactly that. Deciding to accept what fate had given him, Henry settled back into the pillows and mulled over Dom's invitation.

SHOWERED AND FED, Henry sat back in his chair with a sigh. "Thanks for that." When Dom had mentioned breakfast, Henry had pictured cereal or maybe tea and toast. Not the plate of bacon, sourdough toast, poached egg, avocado, and tomatoes that Dom had set before him. "I'd never have thought about having that for brekkie."

Dom glanced at his phone where it sat on the table next to them. "It's half ten. More like brunch." He smiled. "But you're welcome. I like cooking, even more so when it's for someone other than me." He stood and collected Henry's plate. "And it sets you up nicely for the rest of the day."

Henry shot to his feet. "Let me clear up, it's only fair."

"Cheers." Dom took his seat again and watched as Henry pottered about the small kitchen area, tidying up the mess.

The whole thing felt far more intimate than it had any right to.

"*So,*" Dom began, and Henry paused wiping the worktop to

look at him. "I'm going to go for a walk down to the lake in a bit. Did you fancy joining me?" When Henry didn't answer immediately, he added, "Don't feel like you have to."

"I do want to."

Dom's smile was slow building and Henry watched it light up his whole face.

"But I need to go back to my villa and change first." Henry glanced down at yesterday's clothes. He'd showered, but putting yesterday's boxers on wasn't ideal. Oh, who was he kidding? If he'd been on his own, he would've worn the same pair for two days straight and not given a fuck. But he couldn't have Dom thinking he didn't change his bloody underwear. "If you don't mind waiting for me, then I'd love to join you."

Glancing out the window showed another beautiful winter's day and Henry had the sudden urge to be out in the fresh air.

"I'm more than happy to wait for you." Dom stood and walked over to where Henry leant against the worktop and took the cloth out of his hand. "I'll finish up here. You nip back to your villa and do what you need to do."

They stood so close, it was nothing for Henry to lean in and place a soft kiss on Dom's mouth. "Okay." He had no idea what made him do it. Instinct had moved his body closer, and Dom had met him halfway. "I'll go then."

"Yeah." Dom shuffled forwards, pressing his body flush to Henry's, his interest hard to miss. Slipping a hand around Henry's waist and holding his jaw with the other, Dom kissed him, no soft press of lips this time, and Henry moaned into it, winding his arms around Dom's neck.

They kissed and kissed, lazy and unhurried, and Henry shamelessly rubbed himself against the bulge in Dom's jeans. At this rate, he'd have no option but to change his boxers.

"Oh," Henry muttered, eyes going wide as Dom suddenly dropped to his knees and reached for the button on Henry's jeans. "You don't have to do that," he said as Dom unzipped him.

Oh, please god, don't stop.

Dom chuckled as he freed Henry from the confines of his underwear, long fingers wrapping around his length with a sure grip. "Shush and enjoy it."

Henry did as he was told, holding onto the worktop behind him for dear life as Dom went to town on his cock. Warm, wet suction and the flick of a clever tongue made Henry's toes curl and his pulse race. His stomach tightened in anticipation, and he gave into the urge to sink his hands in Dom's hair. "So good," he mumbled, thrusting his hips gently as Dom sucked him down.

With each slide into Dom's mouth, Henry's orgasm edged closer and closer until he couldn't stem the wave of pleasure threatening to overtake him. "Gonna come," he warned, hopefully giving Dom enough time to pull off if he wanted.

Instead, Dom hummed, sending Henry barrelling towards a climax that made his knees weak. His breath came in shallow gasps, and he scrunched his eyes shut tight, clinging onto the feeling of euphoria as Dom swallowed everything he had to give.

"Wow," Henry managed when he finally got his breathing under control. "That was . . . wow."

"Thanks." Dom sat back on his knees, a smug smile in place.

As well he might, Henry mused, feeling wrung out. "Give me a second and I'll return the favour." A glance down at Dom's jeans told him that Dom was more than ready for that to happen. Henry licked his lips, then tugged Dom up to his feet and swapped places.

"My turn." Henry sank to his knees, determined to match Dom's awesome blow job with one of his own.

THIRTY MINUTES and some slightly sore knees later—tiled floors weren't ideal for kneeling on—Henry was on his way back to his own villa for a change of clothes when his phone rang.

Ella.

Of course it was.

Surprised it took her this long to call.

Tapping the phone screen, Henry smirked when his sister's smiling face appeared. "Hey, sis. Fancy hearing from you."

She rolled her eyes. "You're lucky I waited this long to call you." Glancing behind him, her eyes twinkled with amusement. "And you're out for a walk, how nice." Grinning, she asked, "Are you walking to or from somewhere?"

Henry sighed, knowing she'd get the details out of him one way or another. And to be fair, he didn't mind. Ella had been his go-to confidant since they were little. "I'm walking back to my villa." That didn't mean he had to make it easy for her, and her little huff made him smile.

Her eyes narrowed, "Are they last night's clothes you're wearing?" She was fishing and they both knew it.

Shaking his head, Henry fixed her with a pointed look. "I know what you're doing, but as a matter of fact, yes they are."

She squealed so loudly that Henry quickly hugged the phone to his chest, lest she scared small children and animals. After a couple of seconds, he lifted it away and glared at her. "Finished?"

"Sorry." She looked anything but. Smiling at him, she whispered, "Henry West, did you have *sex* last night?"

He glanced around to make sure no unfortunate family happened to be walking nearby and, when convinced the coast was clear, answered, "I might have." His smile was impossible to contain, and he gave up, taking his sister's ribbing in good humour.

"Good for you. I won't ask for details—"

"I wouldn't give you any."

She ignored him. "But you have to tell me what's happening now. Are you seeing him again? Was it a one-off holiday thing? Was the sex good?" She waggled her eyebrows in a way that made her look ridiculous, and Henry laughed.

"I'm meeting him in about half an hour, so not a one-off, but definitely a holiday-only thing, and yes it was."

Ella was quiet while she sorted through his answers, and when her eyebrows scrunched together, he knew what she was going to say next. "Why just a holiday-only thing. If you get on that well, there's no reason why—"

"I've known him for one day."

"But still . . ."

He let out a long-suffering sigh and made it loud enough that Ella heard it. "We're both just out of relationships. We don't live near enough each other to start something and neither of us is looking for anything more than a bit of fun." It was the truth, Henry knew, but the words felt funny on his tongue. He shook it off and pointed a finger at her on his phone. "Take that look off your face. You told me to come away and have fun, and that's exactly what I'm doing. Don't try to make more of it."

After a moment's silence where she glared at him and he glared back, she grudgingly agreed not to press. "Okay. Well, have fun today and I'll talk to you later."

"Bye, sis." He blew a loud kiss at her and made her laugh.

Much better.

They hung up as his villa came into view and Henry stopped suddenly, smiling at the two grey squirrels running about near his front door. They both scarpered when they noticed him, and Henry watched them dart up the nearest tree, making a racket as they went. They weren't all that active at this time of year. Henry remembered reading that they slept a lot more, so he felt even more fortunate at having seen them.

His villa looked as pristine as when he'd first arrived yesterday. Hardly surprising since he'd spent most of his time at Dom's. Henry was no stranger to a holiday romance. He'd had his fair share in his late teens, knew how intense they could feel in the moment. He liked to think he was old enough now to appreciate the feeling was temporary and not let himself get too caught up in it.

Like he'd said to Ella, this was a holiday fling.

Nothing more.

And that suited him just fine.

Stripping off his clothes, Henry found some clean boxers and a fresh T-shirt and pulled them on. Yesterday's jeans were fine, but after a moments deliberation, he changed his socks too.

Mum would be proud.

Once dressed, he texted Dom to let him know he was on his way and set off. They'd agreed to meet at the top of the walkway down to the lake. Dom was already there as Henry walked up. He leant against the wooden railing, looking out on the view below.

Henry took the opportunity to study his profile, commanding even from this far out. Dom didn't have a super-defined six-pack or anything, but he was solid, with wide shoulders that Henry fantasised over a lot.

He had a beanie and gloves on, a testament to the clear but chilly day. Henry smirked; he was dressed much the same. "Hey," Henry said when he was within speaking distance.

Dom turned to him and smiled, the warmth in it tickling Henry's insides. There was something about being greeted like that that made him feel ten feet tall.

"Ready?" Dom asked, gesturing to the walkway stretching out below them.

Henry nodded. "Yeah."

With his hat on, Dom's features seemed more defined, and Henry zeroed in on the scar running through Dom's left eyebrow. He was reaching up to trace a finger over it before he realised. "I never noticed this before."

Dom snorted. "Probably because you weren't looking at my face."

Henry blushed on cue. "I wasn't staring at your dick the whole time," he said just as a couple walked past. They grinned at him, and Henry sighed.

Why me?

Dom's laughter echoed around them, and Henry joined him leaning on the fence, grumbling under his breath. "Fuck's sake."

"That's because you pay no attention to your surroundings."

Henry shrugged. It was a strong possibility. "Maybe." He faced Dom. "Anyway, back to your scar. Can I ask how you got it?"

Dom ran a finger over the small silver line where the hair didn't grow anymore. "I used to have a piercing there."

"Oh, ouch." Henry winced just imagining it.

"Yep." Dom scrunched his nose. "It hurt more coming out than it did going in. Well, the day after, anyway."

Henry could well imagine. "You didn't want another?"

"Nope. I used to play rugby, so I figured maybe getting another piercing wasn't the best idea."

Henry gestured to his eyebrow. "Is that how it came out?"

"Nah." Dom looked sheepish for a moment. "Not exactly. I was with my teammates, but it wasn't on the pitch."

Ahh.

"You were pissed?"

Dom grinned and put his thumb and forefinger an inch apart. "Little bit. My brothers took the piss for weeks." He gestured to the path and Henry nodded, falling into step alongside him.

"So, you mentioned before that you work with your brothers. What do you do and how many do you have?"

"I have two brothers, one older, one younger," Dom said with a smile as they walked down the gently sloping wooden walkway. "Both huge pains in the arse, of course."

Henry grunted in sympathy. "I have a sister like that."

"Oh, how old?"

"Ella's a year older than me." Henry's phone buzzed with a text the minute he said her name.

Like I summoned her.

He imagined Ella suddenly appearing in the middle of a pentagram, or whatever it was people used for these things, and grinned to himself. She'd be all feisty and put upon. It took him a moment to realise Dom was talking. "Sorry, what did you say?" Henry flushed at being caught not listening. "I was busy imagining my sister as a demon."

Dom laughed. "Is she really that bad?"

"No, she's great." He pulled his phone out to show Dom the two unread texts on the screen. "Just nosy."

"Ahh. Well, while you were daydreaming about demon sisters, I was telling you that me and my brothers work at the family garden centre slash café slash Christmas shop at this time of year."

"Oh." That was so not what Henry had imagined him doing for a living. He gave Dom a quick once-over out of the corner of his eye as they walked. Now that he thought about it, yeah, he could picture Dom working outside, hefting heavy plants and bags of compost around. "You must know a lot about plants and shit then?"

Oh my god. Really, Henry?

He should come with a muzzle for times like this.

Dom gave him a quizzical look, which he thoroughly deserved, and Henry nudged him with his shoulder.

"Forget I just said that ridiculous statement. What I meant was that you must . . . um . . ." Words failed him. He knew absolutely nothing about gardening, and Henry wished the wooden planks would part and swallow him whole. "I have no idea."

Fortunately, Dom chuckled and nudged him back. "To answer your *ridiculous statement,* I know a fair bit about plants and shit. Hard not to when you grow up around it all. But I'm more of a jack of all trades. My eldest brother, Simon, is the resident expert. He's got a degree in horticulture—which is wasted working there, in my opinion—but he's happy enough. He also works part time in the gardens at one of the local estates, so I guess he's using his degree in that aspect." He came to an abrupt stop and huffed out a laugh. "And that was way more information than you wanted or needed to know about my family. I'm so sorry."

Henry grinned at him. "I guess I'm not the only one who waffles when nervous."

"I'm not nervous."

"What's your excuse then?" Henry had a moment to wonder if he'd offended him before Dom's wide smile set him at ease again.

"Touché." Dom blew out a breath. "Okay, so I'm not exactly nervous, but I do have something on my mind."

A prickle of apprehension ran down Henry's spine. "Okay."

Dom caught Henry's arm and gently brought them to a stop. He turned and leant on the wooden fence and Henry mirrored his stance. "We're only here for a week, and I don't know about you, but I'd like to make the most of that time. So, I have a proposal for you."

Oh.

Henry liked the sound of this. His lips curled at the edges. He hadn't smiled this much in ages. "Go on."

Dom met his gaze, those piercing green eyes of his capturing Henry's attention and keeping it. "Firstly, please feel free to turn me down flat, I won't be offended. The thing is, I was quite prepared to spend the week on my own, but now that I've met you that's not so appealing any more. I know it'll only be for the next six days, but what do you say to spending them together? No strings. We can do all the things or none of them, I don't care." He slid closer to Henry until their shoulders brushed. "I like you, Henry."

Henry swallowed, mouth suddenly dry as a bone. "I like you too." He didn't even care that it came out all breathy, too caught up in the heat of Dom's gaze.

"I think we'd have a great time. Whatever we end up doing."

Me. Henry thought, licking his lips. *You could end up doing me.*

He didn't need a mirror to know that his cheeks were flushed. Henry felt the heat creep over his skin as his mind dropped to the gutter and filled his head with all the dirty things they could do in a week. He glanced at the tall, beautifully lit Christmas tree still visible at the top of the path and the words spilled out before he could stop them. "Sort of like a no-strings Noel?"

Dom stared at him, as well he might. *Christ Henry.* "Hmm, I guess we are surrounded by all things Christmas." His gaze dropped to Henry's mouth, lingered for a moment, then drifted back up as though drinking Henry in. "Well? What do you think?"

"Yeah." Henry had to clear his throat to get the word out.

"Yeah?" Dom gave him a gentle shoulder bump, grinning widely.

"Yes," Henry repeated, voice a lot steadier this time. His smile must have matched Dom's because it was so wide his cheeks hurt. "I want to spend the week with you."

Dom leant closer to whisper in Henry's ear. "Even if it means walking on swinging planks through the trees?"

Hot breath tickled Henry's ear and he shivered. "Mm-hmm." Then Dom's words registered, and he straightened. "Wait, what?"

"Up there." Dom pointed to the high walkways barely visible through the trees.

"Err . . ." Henry squinted, trying to make out the people.

Dom chuckled beside him. "I'm kidding. I would never try and force you. But you can watch me from the safety of the ground. Okay?"

"How high is it again? And did you say there's a zipwire at the end?" Henry studied the trees again, but they were too far away to make anything out. He didn't fancy being tied to a rope and wobbling about up in the trees, but the zipwire . . . he'd always secretly fancied the idea of that, but his fear of heights stopped him.

"Come with me." Dom tugged on his arm until Henry started walking again.

Their fingers brushed, and Henry took a chance entwining them. His heart raced and he held his breath for Dom's reaction. It was a small thing, they weren't even holding hands properly, but when Dom's palm slid against his, gripping Henry tight, warmth filled his chest and he smiled to himself.

Yeah, doing this for the next week was an awesome idea.

CHAPTER 5

Dom led Henry down the path to the bottom of the hill towards the start of the aerial walkway, hands still clasped together. That had surprised him, pleasantly though. He hadn't expected Henry to be so openly tactile.

You hardly know him, Dom reminded himself.

Something he could remedy over the next few days. He hadn't come out that morning with the intention of asking Henry to spend the week together, but as they were walking and talking, it had suddenly made perfect sense.

They were both here on their own and if last night and this morning were anything to go by, they liked each other's company. Why not spend the week together? It'd save a lot of awkward moments wondering whether to ask Henry to do things or not.

A week with great company and no expectations was exactly what Dom needed. And Henry too, judging by how quickly he'd agreed.

With a new spring in his step, Dom walked over to the gate in front of them. "This is where you start." He pointed to the tree trunk that connected the ground to the first aerial base in the trees. It had a rope suspended above it, about waist height in an adult. "You hold on to that and use it to walk up the tree trunk to the first tree."

"Hmm." Henry eyed it like it was an unexploded bomb.

Tugging on his hand Dom led him along the path, pointing out the various stages. Squeals and laughter sounded up above them as children and adults alike made their way through the course.

"You're attached to the overhead rope and you're wearing a harness. You can't fall off."

"I know that," Henry grumbled.

Dom nudged him playfully. "It's totally fine that you don't fancy it. Don't stress."

"Show me the zipwire bit."

They walked through the trees with Dom pointing out the rest of the course until they came to the end part.

"Wow." Henry looked up, shielding his eyes from the sun. "That looks high."

From where they were stood, it really did.

They watched a couple of people step off the platform and whizz overhead along the zipwire, legs and arms flailing about.

"Fun, though," Dom murmured, excitement building as he thought about doing it himself.

"They look like spiders from down here," Henry mused, still looking up as a particularly gangly bloke passed overhead. "Big, black spiders."

"That's what I'll look like too, then."

Henry's gaze snapped to his. "You definitely gonna do it?"

"Yeah, I think so. Probably book it for Friday afternoon, when it's not so busy."

And you might have gone home.

He didn't say that though. No point wishing their time away. "Come on, I'm going to go book it at the sports place and you can see if there's anything else you fancy doing."

Henry took one last look at the zipwire, then reached for Dom's hand again. Dom looked down at his feet to hide his smile. He didn't want to make a big deal out of something Henry seemed to have done without thinking.

They got the odd look as they walked around the lake, but most people were either too busy doing their own thing or didn't care enough to react. Dom couldn't give a flying fuck what people thought, and he didn't let go of Henry's hand until he absolutely had to.

THE INDOOR SPORTS area was huge.

After booking his slot for the aerial walkway, he gave Henry a tour of everything it had to offer. From the climbing wall to badminton, tennis courts, and finally the rows of snooker and pool tables.

"Anything take your fancy?" Dom spread his arms out, encompassing everything behind them. He was active by nature, and although he'd meant it when he said he'd be happy to go along with whatever Henry did or didn't want to do, he really hoped he'd be up for a few games.

Henry shoved his hands in the pockets of his jeans and rocked back on his heels. "Yeah. There's one or two things I wouldn't mind doing."

"Such as?"

"I've not played since school, but I wouldn't mind a go at badminton or tennis."

"We can do both," Dom blurted, making Henry laugh.

He gestured to what he had on. "I'm not dressed for it at the minute, but we can book something for later in the week if you want?"

"Okay." Dom started walking towards the information desks, keen to get it booked before Henry changed his mind.

"Oh, and pool. We could play that now."

Dom glanced over his shoulder at him. "You any good?"

Henry shrugged. "I'm not bad."

NOT BAD TURNED out to be a gross understatement. Dom liked to think he was quite good at both snooker and pool, but Henry wiped the floor with him. Three games in a row.

"Fuck's sake," he grumbled as he watched the white ball disappear into the hole after his striped one.

Henry laughed, head thrown back, and Dom couldn't help but join in.

"So you lied when I asked if you were any good."

Henry smirked. "I didn't lie, exactly."

"You said, and I quote, 'I'm not bad.'" Dom gestured to the table where he had five balls left to Henry's one. "This will make four games in a row that you've beaten me."

"Damn, we should've made a bet."

The mischief in Henry's expression had Dom instantly intrigued. "What sort of bet?"

"One I probably shouldn't say out loud in present company." He nodded to the tables either side of them, then pulled out his phone.

Dom watched, heart rate steadily increasing as he waited for Henry to finish typing. When his own phone buzzed, Dom almost dropped it in his haste to get it out of his pocket.

Henry: *Whoever wins the next game gets to pick what we do tonight.*

Dom: *Do? As in?*

Henry: *As in gets to pick our activities from 6pm-midnight . ;)*

Oh.

Dom looked up to find Henry staring at him, eyes dark and expression telling Dom exactly what he meant by that.

"Okay." He picked up his cue, then started to gather all the balls into the triangle again. "Who wants to break?"

Henry laughed and gestured for Dom to go first. "You need all the help you can get."

"Nah," Dom said as he leant over the table. "I just needed the right incentive." He smacked the white into the triangle of balls and whooped in delight as he sunk a stripe.

Whether Henry let him win or Dom miraculously improved, he couldn't decide. As his last ball disappeared into the pocket, Dom raised his arms in triumph. "Yes! *Finally.*"

Henry rolled his eyes, but Dom noted he didn't look all that bothered about having lost.

Maybe he likes the idea of you taking control.

Dom immediately pushed that thought to the back of his mind. At least while they were in public, anyway.

"So," Henry said, setting his cue on the table and lowering his voice. "What did you have in mind for later?"

"Hmm." Dom tapped his chin with a finger. "I need to give it some serious thought." That made Henry laugh, and Dom walked over to stand beside him. "But first, why don't we go get some lunch?"

"Yeah, I could eat."

They chose to get a sandwich at the coffee shop inside the sports area, and as they queued for their drinks, Dom marvelled again at how easy this all was. Maybe knowing this was a time-limited experience took some of the pressure off? He didn't have to worry about what this was between them because after this week, they never had to see each other again.

That thought wasn't as comforting as he'd thought it would be.

Because maybe you like him a little more than you're willing to admit. That's why it's easy between the two of you.

Dom huffed to himself. He was being ridiculous. Two days. That's all it had been. Holiday flings were like that, though. He needed to remember that this would all feel different once they got back to real life.

"You okay?" Henry asked, giving him a quizzical look.

"Yeah, just thinking."

"About tonight?" Henry raised his eyebrows. "I know I am."

That brought a smile to Dom's face, and he forced himself to be in the present, to enjoy Henry's company instead of worry about something that was days away yet. "I know exactly what I'm going to do with you," he murmured, just for Henry's ears.

Henry nudged him, playfully. "Oh yeah?"

"Mm-hmm."

"Can't wait."

"WELL." Henry smiled ruefully as he leant on the wooden railing next to Dom and sighed. "As pretty as this all is . . ." He gestured to the fairy lights sparkling in the dark surrounding the outdoor pool. "It's not what I imagined when you won our bet."

Dom knew he was taking a chance suggesting this, but swimming at night here was something he loved, and he wanted to show Henry. Hopefully it wouldn't backfire and ruin their evening. "It is pretty though, right?"

White trees dotted the outside of the pool and along the banks either side of the slides. With the lights illuminated in the water, it had a magical feel, and Dom loved all of it.

"Yes," Henry grudgingly agreed. "It is."

"You can't come here without going in the pool, and at night is the best time."

Henry snorted. "This is day two. We have a whole five days to come here. Why tonight when we could be naked—"

His mouth snapped shut as a family with small children walked past them, kids yawning loudly.

"When we could be doing other things?" Dom finished for

him. He nodded, and Dom leant in close to whisper, "Plenty of time for that later."

With a put-upon sigh, Henry slung his rucksack over his shoulder. "Come on, then, let's get this over with."

He started to walk down the path towards the entrance, but Dom reached for his arm, suddenly not so sure he'd made the right choice. Swimming wasn't everyone's idea of fun. "We don't have to go swimming if you don't want to. I know it's not—"

"Hey." Henry turned to face him fully and held Dom's hand, their gloved fingers mostly covered by their coat sleeves. "I was kidding. I'm sorry if I sounded like a whiny arse. This is a great idea."

"You sure?" Dom wasn't convinced.

"Who doesn't love a water slide? And the place does look gorgeous." Henry gave his fingers a squeeze before glancing around them, then leaning in for a quick kiss. "I just want to get you naked again, that's all." He adjusted his backpack and grimaced. "And seeing you in your shorts is going to be a huge fucking tease."

Dom smiled, relief chasing away the doubts from earlier. "Think of it as foreplay," he whispered, and Henry barked out a laugh.

"That'll just make it worse," he exclaimed, slapping Dom's shoulder in mock outrage. "And there'll be hundreds of people in there to watch. What sort of monster are you?"

"Christ, I didn't mean it like that." Dom huffed, flustered.

"I know, sorry." Henry bumped shoulders with him, laughing softly. "Come on. Show me what's so special about this bloody pool."

Once inside, they paused to take off their coats, hats, and gloves as the heat hit them.

Henry ran a hand through his hair, trying to tame it. "I forgot how hot it is in here."

"It'd be a bit shit if it was cold." Dom grinned at Henry's eye-roll. As they walked along the path circling down to the pool area, he pointed out the various restaurants and what food they served. "If you fancied it, we could try a few out this week?"

Henry side-eyed him. "You mean you've not brought enough food for every meal?"

"No." It was Dom's turn to roll his eyes. "Only the first night and brekkie."

"Well, as you know, I had nothing, so eating out would be good." Henry winced, and Dom didn't think it was solely the heat making his cheeks that pink. "But maybe stick to the cheaper ones. I am a poor ex-student after all."

"None of them are all that cheap here." Which was why Dom tried to cook at the villa for most of his stay. What had possessed him to suggest they try a *few*? "To be honest, I usually cook a lot when I come here, so why don't we do that. Maybe pick one restaurant to go to, then get the rest from the shop."

Henry visibly relaxed at that suggestion. "Yeah, sounds good."

They parted ways inside the changing rooms, finding cubicles across from each other to get changed into their swimming gear.

Dom was waiting for Henry by the lockers when he came out. He might've already seen Henry naked, but that didn't alter the fact that Henry in a pair of low-slung swimming shorts was a lovely sight. All long limbs dusted with dark hair.

Dom felt the stirrings of desire low in his belly and conjured up all the horrible thoughts he could muster to ward it off.

Maybe this wasn't such a good idea after all!

"Ready?" Henry bounced on the balls of his feet, his obvious excitement pulling a smile from Dom and helped drag his thoughts out of the gutter.

"Yeah, come on."

They walked through the showers and came out into the huge area that housed the main pool, the kids area, slides, a snack bar, and various seating dotted throughout. The lighting was muted, darkness visible through the huge glass dome above. This was

Dom's favourite time to come swimming. Fewer families about, fewer people in general, and there was something magical about swimming outside at night, especially with the addition of all the Christmas lights.

"Wow." Henry stopped just inside the entrance, mouth open as he took it all in. "I've seen the pictures, obviously, but it's bigger than I was expecting."

Dom elbowed him gently. "Better too?"

He flashed Dom a smirk. "Bigger is always better."

"Right." On that note, they needed to get in the water and off the topic of anything remotely sexual. "This way."

"I thought we were going outside?" Henry pointed to the sign indicating the outdoor pool was in the other direction.

"Yeah, but if you go outside straight away, the water will feel cold. You need to go in the big indoor pool first."

"Why?" Henry asked, his confusion clear to see.

"Trust me, okay? I speak from experience."

Looking utterly unconvinced, Henry shrugged and followed Dom to the shallow steps of the big pool.

The air inside the swimming area was warm, so the water in the main pool area always came as a bit of a shock, especially when you were virtually dry. Dom strode purposely through the shallow end, laughing at Henry's muttered curses behind him.

"Why is it so bloody cold?"

Dom turned and walked backwards. "Because you're warm."

"Not any more I'm not," Henry grumbled, wincing as they got waist deep.

"Come swim for a bit, you'll soon get used to it." Dom ducked under the rope separating the shallow area from the deeper water and swam over to the far end.

When he reached the wall, he stopped and turned back the way he'd come, wiping the water from his eyes.

Henry wasn't far behind him, arms cutting through the water in an almost perfect front crawl.

I bet that's where he gets his toned body from.

"You swim a lot, then?" Dom asked as Henry trod water next to him.

"I used to. Not so much anymore."

"How come?"

Henry shrugged a shoulder, not an easy feat while keeping himself afloat. "Not enough time." He didn't seem keen to elaborate, so Dom let it drop.

"Race you to the other side." Dom set off like a rocket, smiling to himself as he imagined Henry's outraged face.

He touched the wall first, but Henry was hot on his heels, closer than Dom anticipated, and as he turned around, he was met with a face full of water. "Oi," he spluttered, hanging onto the narrow ledge next to him.

"That's for cheating." Henry smiled with smug satisfaction.

Fair enough.

Dom raised a hand. "Truce?" He really didn't want another face full.

"I suppose." Henry floated on his back for a moment, staring up at the ceiling smiling. "Look, you can see us."

Dom looked up at their reflections, as clear as day above them. They were the only two in the deep end of the main pool, and looking at all the empty water surrounding them, it felt like they were the last two people on earth. Dom smiled, ignoring the funny feeling in his stomach.

It's just for the week.

"I think that's enough adjusting to the temperature," he said, pushing off from the side. "Let's go outside."

They swam across to the steps tucked in round the corner and used the rope bannister to pull themselves up.

"Fuck me, it's cold once you get out." Henry shivered, and Dom laughed at him.

"So delicate."

"Piss off." Henry nudged him with his shoulder. "I can see the goosebumps on your arms."

Dom shrugged, because yeah, it was cold. "It'll make the outside pool feel that much warmer, trust me."

"Hmm."

They walked up the slope to the entrance to the outside pool, draughts of the chill night air seeping through the plastic curtains separating the inside and outside.

"Christ." Henry shivered again, and Dom agreed with him this time.

"I know, but it's worth it."

He led the way to the steps and sighed in pleasure as soon as his feet hit the warm water.

"Ooh. That's nice."

"Told you."

They swam through the plastic partitions and out into the warm water of the outside pool. Steam rose from the surface, the underwater lighting giving it a magical feel, and fairy lights covered Christmas trees decorating the grass surrounding it.

So pretty.

"I see what you mean." Henry ducked under the water until only his head remained above it and glanced around them.

Warmth filled him and Dom beamed, thrilled that Henry seemed to like it as much as he did. Not that he would've said anything if Henry hadn't been impressed, but he'd have been disappointed for sure.

They weren't alone out there, but it wasn't overly busy either. A couple cuddled in the corner of the pool, and the pang of jealousy took Dom by surprise. Even if he would've been here with Sam, they wouldn't have been doing that. And not that he wished he and Sam were back together, but he did miss the closeness of having a partner who knew the real you. The parts that friends and family sometimes didn't get to see.

Yeah, he missed that. Especially at this time of year.

"Hey, you all right?" Henry's bright smile pulled him back to the present, and Dom returned it easily.

They might not know each other well, but they were here together, and getting to know someone new was equally as special.

I need to focus on that. Make the most of this week and not dwell on what I don't have.

"Yeah, sorry. Just zoned out for a sec."

"Oh? Thinking about anything in particular?" He waggled his eyebrows suggestively, and Dom huffed out a laugh, gaze darting below the water.

"Well, I wasn't, but I am now. Thanks for that." Dom needed a distraction fast. "You fancy a go down the river rapids?"

Henry glanced over to the mini waterfall to their right. "Over there?"

"Yeah. Come on, it's fun." Dom waited a beat. "I'll race you." He set off at speed, but Henry was ready for him this time, and they reached the start of the river rapids at the same time.

Dom hauled himself up and over the low barrier separating the rapids from the pool, the cold air hitting his skin and making him gasp, the cool spray of the mini waterfalls adding to it. Jeez, he'd forgotten how fucking freezing the start bit was.

Henry tumbled over after him, landing half on top of him, laughing, and Dom wiggled away, pulling himself along, heading towards the first slide.

The water here was about a foot deep and the current carried him round the corner and headfirst into the first gentle whirlpool. He hurried to half swim, half pull himself along to one of the two long slides that were the main attraction.

He got to the top fractionally ahead of Henry and disappeared over the edge, feet first and lying down on his back for extra speed. Hitting the water hard, it whooshed over his head and the current whipped him round past the exit point and Dom found himself going around again. He watched helpless as Henry whizzed round the corner and out of sight, his loud laughter ringing out into the night.

Bastard. Dom gritted his teeth, then grinned as he caught the edge of the whirlpool and lunged after Henry.

They both got caught in the next one. Dom landed practically in Henry's lap, both of them disappearing under the water for a second before spluttering to the surface amid raucous laughter.

"Oh my god, get off me," Henry sputtered, face splitting with a huge smile. They managed to untangle themselves but ended up going round one more time before finally getting free.

When they spilled out into the pool at the end, they were both out of breath and grinning like idiots. Henry pulled himself up the metal ladder, water cascading over his back and shoulders, shorts clinging to his slim hips like a second skin.

Dom swallowed, averting his eyes and forcing away all the inappropriate thoughts threatening to surface.

Time to go.

"Want to go again?" Henry asked, wiping water out of his eyes and smiling like the Cheshire cat.

Dom took his time climbing the ladder, heart racing as he stood and looked Henry in the eye. "No. I think we should go."

"What?" Henry frowned. "I thought—" A slow, dirty smile appeared as Dom dropped his gaze to Henry's crotch, then back up, eyebrows raised. "Yeah, I'm done."

"Thought so." Dom walked past him, biting his lip as their bare shoulders brushed. "Come on."

They walked as quickly as they dared on the wet stones around the pool, neither of them speaking until they reached the entrance to the showers. Normally Dom would've grabbed his shampoo and washed the chlorine out of his hair, save him doing it later, but not tonight.

Tonight he wanted to get back to the villa as fast as humanly possible.

"Just rinse off," he whispered in Henry's ear. "We can shower at mine."

Henry shook his head, eyes dark as he backed under the nearest shower head. "Mine's closer."

Dom nodded. "Perfect."

They got dressed in record time. Dom was barely dry as he pulled his clothes on and said a silent prayer of thanks that he'd chosen to wear trackie bottoms and not jeans. Slinging his rucksack over his shoulder, he hurried out of the changing area to find Henry already waiting by the doors, a lazy grin in place.

"Did you bother drying off at all?" Dom asked, reaching up to flick the ends of Henry's wet hair as it dripped into his face.

Henry shrugged. "Enough to get my clothes on." He pushed off the wall and marched ahead through the double doors, Dom chuckling as he hurried to catch up.

"We don't need to run back," Dom said as he reached him.

"It's nine thirty." Henry muttered. "That means you still have two and a half hours to choose what activities we do." He glanced at Dom. "I don't want to waste one second of it." The heat in his eyes stole Dom's breath and he tripped over his feet. "Steady." Henry caught his arm, keeping him upright, soft laughter tickling Dom's ear as he fell against him. "Don't want you injuring yourself before the main event."

"Stop with all the pressure," Dom grumbled, "I'll get stage fright."

Henry laughed. "Don't worry. I'll help you with that." He leant in close to whisper in his ear. "You can tell me exactly what to do."

"Stop talking. These trackies hide nothing." Dom tugged at the bottom of his coat, hoping he wasn't about to get kicked out for indecent behaviour. "And walk quicker."

"You just told me to slow down."

"I take it back."

Henry shook his head but dutifully matched Dom's pace as

they hurried up the path and eventually out into the cool night air. "Thank fuck for that," he said as they headed for the steps. "I was melting in this bloody coat."

"Same." Dom pulled his beanie on, covering his wet hair, even though he was sweating. He reached for Henry's hand without thinking, only realising what he'd done as their fingers slid together. "Oh, sorry," he said, dropping his hand. "Force of habit."

Henry grabbed his hand back, linking their fingers again and holding tight. "I like it." His smile was shy, hesitant, when he glanced at Dom. "If you do?"

"Yeah," Dom gave a small, shy smile of his own. "I do." It felt right, like he'd known Henry forever instead of the two days it actually had been. They might have spent nearly all of those two days together, but they were making the most of their shitty situations, not embarking on a lasting relationship. Holding hands like this had no right to feel as easy as it did, though.

They walked back in comfortable silence. Dom's thoughts swirled as he tried to make sense of something he should probably just accept for what it was and enjoy.

Seven days.

That's all they were sharing.

He and Henry were both still hurting from failed relationships of their own. Neither of them was looking for more.

This was a bit of fun.

Nothing else.

Careful, Dom. Don't scare him by reading more into this than there is.

"All right?" Henry asked as they turned into the road for his villa.

"Yeah, just thinking."

Henry snorted. "Well, stop it. Nothing good ever comes from that."

He was more right than he realised. Dom shook it off and concentrated on the present.

Henry and their evening together.

Where I get to call the shots.

There, that was a much more appealing train of thought.

Henry pulled a key out of his pocket and gestured to the villa to their right. "This is me." He led the way up the path and unlocked the door, Dom hot on his heels.

Flicking on the light switch, Henry turned to face Dom. He let his bag drop to the ground. "Well?" he asked, leaning back against the wall.

"Well, what?" Dom set his own bag down and kicked off his shoes.

"What are we doing now. You get to decide, remember?"

How could I forget?

"Shower," Dom said, taking off his coat and hanging it up on a peg. Henry did the same, gaze locked on Dom's.

"And then what?"

"We'll see how much energy we've got left."

Henry raised an eyebrow but didn't comment. Instead, he pulled his T-shirt over his head, turned, gifting Dom a view of his glorious shoulders and back, and disappeared into the bedroom.

Moments later the shower turned on and Dom shook himself into action, tugging his own top off as he hurried after Henry.

"Fuck me." Dom stopped inside the doorway to the en suite, drinking in the view of a bare-arsed Henry bending down to pull off his trackies and underwear.

Henry kicked his clothes to the side and straightened, unashamed in his nakedness. "Is that a request?" His cock hung half-hard, and he reached for it, giving himself a couple of leisurely strokes.

Dom almost swallowed his tongue. "Maybe later." Henry looked surprised by that, so Dom shrugged a shoulder. "I like it both ways."

"Good to know." Henry stalked towards him, hands snaking around Dom's waist as he drew him in for a kiss. His tongue found Dom's as he gripped the waistband of Dom's sweats, pushing them over his arse.

The kiss deepened, and Dom slid his hands over Henry's chest, loving the feel of all that smooth skin dusted with dark hair. "Shower," he murmured, his voice trailing off into a moan as Henry squeezed his arse cheeks, fingers slipping between them.

"Take these off then." Henry pushed Dom's sweats further down until they fell to his feet, and Dom stepped out of them, kicking them to the side. Taking his hand, Henry climbed into the shower and Dom followed.

Water cascaded over them, the shower big enough to wet them both.

Henry's hair looked almost black, eyes dark as he placed Dom's hand on his cock, now hard and jutting out in front of him. "What now?" Henry whispered, tongue slipping out to lick his lips.

Dom curled his fingers around Henry's length. As much as he wanted to keep jacking him off, he wanted something else more. His gaze dropped to Henry's mouth and Henry grinned.

Without Dom having to say a word, Henry carefully dropped to his knees, hands on Dom's hips to steady himself.

"This okay?" Dom asked, slotting his fingers into Henry's hair.

"Yeah." Henry looked up, and Dom's stomach clenched at the heat reflected back at him. Gripping the base of Dom's cock, Henry leant forward and took him into his mouth. Wet heat engulfed him, and Dom gasped, fingers curling tight around Henry's hair.

With one hand braced on the shower wall for support, Dom watched as Henry gave him one of the best blow jobs he'd ever had. His tongue teased the underside of Dom's cock, his lips tight as he sucked him into his mouth and then pulled off, only to do it again and again, until Dom was gasping and muttering Henry's name.

"Gonna come."

Henry slid a hand round and over Dom's arse, dipping in between his cheeks. When his finger rubbed over Dom's hole, he shuddered, biting his lip, and pleasure gripped him low in his belly. Henry pushed the tip inside, and that was it. Game over.

Dom came with a groan, hips pushing forward as he shot down Henry's throat.

Fuck me.

Dom's heart hammered against his ribcage, his body all boneless and relaxed in a way only an orgasm could achieve. Henry glanced up at him, still on his knees with his hand fisting his cock. "Come up here."

He helped Henry to his feet, pushed him against the tiled wall, and kissed him hard, his tongue thrusting into Henry's mouth and tasting himself there. Henry moaned as Dom wrapped a hand over his. Together they stroked his cock, Henry's head falling onto Dom's shoulder as Dom took over.

"Close," Henry mumbled, hands finding Dom's shoulders, fingers digging in as he clung on. A couple more strokes was all it took before Henry shuddered.

"*Fuck.*"

Henry's cock pulsed in Dom's hand, come painting his belly before being washed away by the water raining down on them.

They took a moment to catch their breath, then Henry's soft chuckle filled the air.

Dom grunted. "What's so funny?"

"I'm so fucking glad I let you win at pool."

"I knew it!" Dom smacked him lightly on the arse.

Henry leant into him, and Dom wrapped his arms around him to support him. "I have the best ideas."

"You do."

They stayed that way for a few moments longer, until Dom reached behind him to turn off the shower. As much as he didn't want to move from where he stood with Henry pressed against him, a day's worth of activities was starting to catch up with him and his body was heavy with lethargy.

"I can't move," Henry murmured, face smooshed into Dom's neck.

Dom laughed. "I know, me neither, but I can't stand up for much longer. And I'm starving."

On cue, Henry's belly rumbled so loudly it had them both chuckling.

"Yes, food." Henry pushed open the shower door and stepped out. He handed Dom a towel and they quickly dried off, both dressing in their clothes from earlier.

They ate pizza that Henry had picked up from the shop and sat on the sofa watching whatever on the TV.

Exhausted and full, Dom settled back into the cushions, half leaning on Henry, and listened as he commented on the merits of *Strictly Come Dancing*, eyes drifting closed.

He smiled to himself.

I could get used to this.

CHAPTER 6

"Dom." Henry gently shook his shoulder but got no response. He chuckled. Dom was dead to the world.

Not that Henry was faring much better. His whole body felt heavy, eyelids doing their best to drop shut, but he knew if he fell asleep on the sofa, he'd regret it in a few hours when he woke with a stiff neck and back.

"*Dom.*" He tried again, voice a little louder this time, and Dom moaned in response, nose scrunching up and looking way too cute. "Come on, let's go to bed."

"Time's it?" Dom opened his eyes, taking a moment to focus on Henry's face.

"Half-past twelve."

"Damn." Dom pushed himself up into a sitting position and rubbed a hand over his face. "I wanted to have my wicked way with you."

Henry smiled and stood, holding out a hand to him. "You can have your wicked way with me in the morning. Let's go to bed."

Dom swayed when he got to his feet, and Henry was quick to steady him with a hand around his waist. "Thanks," he murmured, a huge yawn cutting off the end of the word. Then his gaze locked with Henry's and he seemed way more alert all of a sudden. "Is this okay? I can go back to my villa if you'd rather."

Henry had just assumed that Dom was staying. Asking him to leave hadn't crossed his mind once. "Do you want to go?"

"No." Dom replied so quickly it made Henry smile.

"Bed then."

They undressed to their undies, the room warm enough not to warrant anything else, and slipped under the covers.

Dom settled onto his side straight away, his breathing evening out, whereas Henry lay on his back, unsure of the etiquette now they were just going to sleep. Drifting off after sex was fine. Henry was generally too knackered to stress over whether cuddling was okay or not.

But this felt different. He didn't know Dom well enough to just snuggle up behind him and put an arm around his waist like he wanted to.

Would it be welcome? Or would it make things awkward?

Not that Henry could feel anymore awkward than he already did.

"What's wrong?" Dom's gravelly voice startled him.

Not asleep then.

"Nothing."

"Mm-hmm." Dom rolled over onto his other side, facing Henry, and Henry felt his gaze even in the dark. "I can hear your mind working overtime and you're lying flat on your back staring at the ceiling."

"I have my eyes closed," Henry lied.

"Of course you do."

Strong fingers wrapped around Henry's left hand, and Henry sighed. "I don't know what to do."

"About what?"

Christ, why didn't I just turn over and go to sleep like a normal person.

He huffed out a breath. Might as well come out with it, Dom

probably already thought he was a weirdo. "I want to cuddle you, but I'm not sure if that's something you'd want so I'm lying here debating what to do about it."

"I see." He squeezed Henry's fingers, then slowly stroked his thumb over the back of Henry's hand. "You could just ask me."

When he said it like that, Henry felt incredibly foolish, and every one of the six years separating them in age seemed to stand out and mock him.

He's so much better at this than me.

"Hey." Dom tugged on his hand until Henry gave in and rolled onto his side to face him. "I get that this whole thing between us is a bit strange. We barely know each other, yet we've spent so much time together I feel like I've known you for weeks, not days."

Henry's eyes had adjusted to the dark enough for him to make out Dom's smile. "Same."

"Then why is it so hard to ask me if I want a cuddle?"

Because I'm a weirdo, obviously. "I don't know."

"Try it. I won't bite."

Henry resisted making a comment, barely. But this wasn't the moment for dirty jokes. Swallowing back nerves that had sprung up from nowhere, Henry whispered, "Is it okay if I cuddle you to sleep?"

"Yeah." Dom turned over without another word, but when Henry failed to move quickly enough, added, "Would it help if I gave you another blow job?" He yawned at the end of the sentence and Henry laughed, tension leaving him in a whoosh.

"As appealing as that sounds, I think I'm good." And he was, whether he'd meant to or not, Dom had broken through whatever was going on in Henry's head and he scooted closer to him, wrapping an arm around his waist like it was something he did every night.

Dom hummed in approval, pressing back into Henry, and

finally Henry settled into something that resembled a relaxed state.

He drifted off to sleep, nose tucked in the back of Dom's neck and a smile tugging at his lips.

RAIN PELTED AGAINST THE WINDOW, waking Henry from the best dream he'd had in ages. He groaned as he rolled onto his back and reached down to adjust his cock, the remnants of his dream leaving him hard and aching.

"Morning."

Henry startled at Dom's chuckle, flushing at being caught with his hand down his pants, and opened his eyes to see Dom sat up against the pillows, phone in hand. "Hey." Dom's gaze dropped to the bulge under the quilt, where Henry had hold of his dick, and he licked his lips.

Henry smirked and gave himself a couple of strokes, making sure Dom saw him do it. "How long have you been up?"

"Not as long as you, by the looks of it." He set his phone aside and shuffled down the bed until he lay next to Henry again. "Need a hand with that?"

Henry opened his mouth to say *yes, obviously*, but his phone rang, vibrating on the bedside table, his sister's name displayed on the screen. He reached over to silence the call and turned back to Dom. "Where were we?"

It rang again.

Jesus, Ella.

Henry groaned and shot Dom an apologetic look. "Sorry. She won't go away until I answer."

"It's fine. I'm going to go get a drink anyway. Tea?"

Henry nodded and sighed as Dom got out of bed and headed into the kitchen. Snatching up his phone, he answered Ella's FaceTime call with a frown.

Ella grinned at him. "Oh, still not a morning person I see."

"Why are you calling so early?" He checked the time. Oh, 9.45. Much later than he'd thought it was.

Her eyes narrowed, and Henry quickly angled the phone so it didn't show the other side of the bed, but it was too late. "Did I interrupt something?"

"Maybe," he hedged, not wanting to go into detail with Dom only in the next room.

"Sorry," she mouthed. "Is he still there?"

"Yep."

"Okay, well, I was just checking you were still alive. I'll let you go, and talk later." She hung up before he had a chance to say goodbye.

But his phone pinged with a text a minute later.

Ella: *Sorry, bro. Glad you're having fun. Talk later. xx*

Henry: *ok x*

Dom came back into the room carrying a tray with two mugs of tea and a plate of toast. He raised an eyebrow. "Finished?"

"Yeah, it was my sister. I'll talk to her later."

Dom set the tray on the bed, and carefully got back in. Henry helped himself to a tea and a piece of toast. "Thanks," he mumbled around a mouthful, suddenly starving.

Dom sipped his tea, watching Henry thoughtfully. "Are you close?"

"Yeah, she's only a year older than me. Our parents moved back up north a few years ago, so it's just us down here now."

Dom smiled and took a bite of his toast.

They'd not really talked about anything in the outside world. Henry had wondered if that was a conscious thing on both their parts. Keep this simple, a holiday fling. They didn't need to know much about each other for that. But Henry was curious. He wondered if Dom was too.

"Are you close with your brothers?"

Dom huffed. "Far too close, sometimes. Working with family

has its pros and cons, but at least we don't all live together anymore." He gave Henry a wry smile. "We've had a few hairy moments."

"Are they big like you?"

"Yeah. We take after my dad."

Henry tried to imagine Dom and his brothers getting into fights and winced. "Where do you live now then?" he asked without thinking.

Dom gave him a curious look, and Henry was suddenly aware they'd ventured into very personal territory. "I bought a house in a village about ten minutes' drive from the garden centre."

He hadn't expected Dom to give him his address or anything, but not even the name of the village? He tried not to let it bother him.

You hardly know each other, remember?

Sat in his bed eating toast wearing nothing but their underwear, Henry was having trouble doing just that.

Maybe Dom caught onto how Henry was feeling because he set his mug down and leant back against the pillows. "The village is Little Choreton, and I actually bought the house with my ex-fiancé."

Henry stared at him, unsure of what to say to that. Kyle was his first serious relationship, and look how that turned out. "What happened? You don't have to answer, sorry. It's none of my business," he added quickly, not wanting to piss Dom off. He was way too curious for his own good.

"No, it's fine. It was a few years ago now." He smiled. "I was your age, actually."

Christ, Henry couldn't imagine buying a house let alone getting married.

Dom sighed. "We bought the house and I think it all caught up to him. He wasn't ready, for any of it." He shrugged. "He left and I stayed."

Henry was a little lost for words. "I'm sorry."

"It's okay, really. Probably the best thing for both of us in the end." He ran a hand through his hair. "I didn't mean to get all heavy on you."

"It was me who asked."

"True." Dom smiled, some of the tension dissipating. "So, now you know all about me. Where do you live?"

Henry felt the colour drain from his face. "Um . . . in Bristol." No way was he about to admit he shared with three of his mates. Not when Dom had bought a house at his age, for fuck's sake. Henry didn't even live on his own. "It's nothing as nice as your house in Little Choreton." Quickly changing the subject, Henry pointed to the rain still battering the windows. "Weather's a bit shite today. What did you fancy doing?"

If Dom thought it odd how quickly he'd switched topics, he didn't say. Instead, he put both their cups back on the tray and then set it on the floor. "I have a few ideas."

"Oh?" Henry liked this turn of events. Liked it a lot. He was more than happy to forget about their conversation as Dom crawled across the bed towards him. "I take it none of them involve leaving this bed?"

Dom's laughter was infectious, and Henry found himself smiling. "We can go out later, but I get to decide what we do now, right? You said so yourself last night."

"I did." He lay back on the pillows and spread his arms wide. "I'm all yours."

Dom's grin turned feral, eyes heavy lidded as he took Henry in from head to toe. He licked his lips and Henry shivered. "Get comfortable. I'm gonna take my time."

THREE HOURS later they ventured outside for food, a game of pool, then back to Henry's villa again for the rest of the night.

And that was pretty much how they spent the next few days.

A walk in the mornings, a game of badminton or pool, plenty of food, and lots and lots of sex.

So much sex, Henry was surprised either of them had the energy to do anything else.

He lost track of the days, one blending into the next, and Thursday came round way too soon.

Their last day together.

Henry woke up in Dom's bed early Thursday morning to one thought only.

Where has the fucking time gone?

Sunlight filtered through the gap in the curtains, promising a beautiful winter's day, but Henry found it hard to appreciate it as the crushing realisation sank in.

They had one more day together then back to their real lives. Back to work and living in a shared house. Not that Henry disliked living with his mates. They all got on great, but a week of having his own space had spoiled him.

And then there was Dom.

Henry glanced over to where he still slept soundly, messy blond hair splayed out across the pillow, darker stubble coating his jaw. The past six days had passed so quickly, and yet Henry felt like they'd been here forever, trapped in their own little bubble.

No part of him wanted to give this up, but deep down he knew it would never work. They had totally different lives. Dom owned his own house, had done for a while, and had a job that he actually enjoyed. He was successful in a way Henry only dreamt about.

I work in a job I sometimes hate, for mediocre pay, and share a house with three blokes like I have for the past four years.

Yes, he'd been putting himself through uni, but even that felt a bit like failure since he'd waited five years to go.

Stop it, he chided.

Just because he wasn't as accomplished as Dom, didn't make

him less. But it did make seeing Dom after this week impossible. Well, unlikely, not impossible.

They'd shared a wonderful week, Henry had loved every second of their time together and he wouldn't trade it for anything, but they were equals here. Locked away from the real world, Henry had none of his real-life pressures weighing him down. He could enjoy Dom's company and not worry about anything other than whether or not they were going out to eat or staying in.

That would all change when they left here. He didn't want Dom to see what a fucking shambles his life was at the minute. Henry wasn't where he wanted to be.

Yet.

And he didn't want Dom's opinion of him to change when he realised that Henry in no way had his life together. Kyle had made him feel embarrassed about his job and living situation. He saw that clearly now, even if he hadn't realised at the time.

And not that Dom and Kyle were anything alike, but Henry wanted to keep this week perfect. He didn't want to tarnish it by having Dom look at him like he was suddenly a disappointment.

And, of course, all that was assuming Dom would even want to see him again after this.

Henry laughed to himself. *Way to get ahead of yourself.*

Dom was probably quite happy to leave tomorrow and never hear from Henry again. That left a sharp stab of *something* in his chest, and Henry rubbed at it absently.

A hand snaked around his waist, followed by the rest of Dom snuggling closer. Henry smiled despite the turmoil raging inside him. He had one day left. Well, one and a half if they stayed late tomorrow, and he was determined to wring every last second out of it.

Starting now.

With Dom's breath tickling his neck and his body a warm

weight pressed up against his side, Henry reached for his phone to do something he'd been thinking about all week.

He went onto the holiday park website and found the activities booking page. A quick scroll down and he clicked on the booking page for the aerial walkway.

Dom had his booked for 3pm tomorrow, and with any luck—

"Fuck." Henry stared at the *Fully Booked* next to the 3pm slot and his heart sank. He'd finally decided to take the plunge and accompany Dom as one last thing to do together, and he'd left it too fucking late. "Bastard arseholes."

A low chuckle sounded beside him and Henry flinched. "Sorry," he said, setting his phone face down on the bedside table and twisting in Dom's hold to face him. "Didn't mean to wake you."

"It's fine," Dom mumbled, yawning. "I don't want to waste our last day sleeping." He pushed a leg between Henry's thighs and scooted closer, kissing the base of Henry's throat and making him moan. "What's got you so cross, anyway?"

"Nothing, really." Henry closed his eyes, enjoying Dom's slow exploration of his neck and throat.

"You sure? It sounded like something had pissed you off big time."

His hand roamed lower, trailing teasing fingers over Henry's cock, and Henry groaned, hips pushing upward. "The aerial walkway was all booked," he muttered without thinking.

Dom stopped what he was doing, propped himself up on one elbow, and stared down at him. "When were you trying to book it for?"

Ah, fuck.

Henry hadn't meant to say that. Now he was just embarrassed. He scrubbed a hand over his face, then sighed in resignation. "Tomorrow with you. But it's fine. I'd probably have hated it anyway." He smiled, but it was weak, at best.

Dom bit his lip, colour covering his cheeks, and Henry

wondered what on earth *he* had to be embarrassed about. "I, um . . . I actually booked two slots for tomorrow."

Henry gaped at him. Had he planned to go with someone else?

Well, fuck me.

Rolling his eyes, Dom punched him on the arm.

"Ow, what was that for?" Henry groused, rubbing his shoulder, not that it had hurt.

"Because I can tell what you're thinking. I booked the other slot on the off chance you changed your mind." He shrugged a shoulder, reaching out to put his hand over Henry's. "Wishful thinking, I know, but . . ."

"Oh." Henry swallowed.

Shit. Now I really have to do it with him.

"So, if you still fancy joining me tomorrow, you can."

"Um . . ."

Dom barked out a laugh. "Only if you want to, Henry. I won't hold it against you."

"But you've already paid." *God, it was like Kyle and the skiing trip all over again.*

Dom, ever perceptive, cupped Henry's face and gently coaxed him to face him. "That's right. *I* paid. That was my decision, not yours. If you want to join me, then that would be fantastic—I'll look after you, I promise—but if you don't want to do it, then that's absolutely fine too. You can watch my spider-like legs as I flail down the zipwire."

Henry snorted. Like Dom would flail doing anything. He'd probably glide down like a member of Cirque du Soleil. But one thing he knew for sure? Dom was nothing like Kyle. Henry felt guilty for ever comparing them.

"Yes."

"Yes?" Dom cocked an eyebrow.

"I'll do the aerial thingy with you, if that's okay?" Henry

realised he'd not actually asked if Dom wanted company, but he'd bought him a ticket, right? So he must do.

Dom beamed, answering Henry's unspoken question. "Yes, of course it's okay. I was hoping you might change your mind. He huffed out a laugh. "Obviously, since I bought an extra ticket."

"Which I'll pay you back for."

"There's no need to—"

"I want to," Henry insisted, and something in his tone must have clued Dom into the fact he was serious.

"Okay." Dom leant in and kissed him, soft lips a sharp contrast to the six-day stubble of his jaw and Henry sighed into it. "What do you want to do today?"

Stay here and pretend we aren't leaving tomorrow.

"Um . . ." Henry shook off the feeling, hoping Dom wouldn't notice. "We could go for a bike ride?" Dom had persuaded him that hiring bikes for the week was a good thing, and to be fair, it did make it quicker to get around. Henry had forgotten how much fun it could be.

"Hmm . . ." Dom moved to kiss his jaw, then his neck, and Henry tilted his head with a hum of pleasure, inviting Dom to have at it. "We could do that."

He moved to lie over Henry, slotting into place between Henry's thighs like he belonged. Sure of his welcome and like there was no place else he'd rather be.

Henry smiled, eyes drifting shut as Dom started up a slow, dirty grind.

"We don't have to go out just yet though," he whispered between kisses, hands sliding under Henry's shoulders to hold him in place.

"Yeah." Henry bucked his hips, meeting every roll of Dom's, pleasure a slow build inside him. "I'm in no rush."

They kissed and kissed, heat coursing through Henry's veins with every lazy sweep of Dom's tongue and every press of his cock against Henry's. They took their time, letting the heat build between them like a slow-burning fire. Henry's hands had a mind of their own, stroking down Dom's broad back, enjoying the bunch and release of his muscles as he moved over him. Eventually they landed on Dom's arse, and he couldn't resist grabbing a handful and squeezing, pulling Dom hard against him.

Dom grunted, pace picking up, and Henry felt the tell-tale sensation in his groin. He hadn't come like that in a good few years, but there was no doubt he was well on his way. Dom's hot breath hit his ear and Henry shivered, needy moans escaping as he tried to get Dom closer still. They rutted against each other, chasing release, and even with two layers of underwear between them, it felt fantastic. Dom held him tight, head buried in the crook of his neck, and Henry gave in to the pleasure threatening to overtake him. With his head pushed back against the pillow, he came with a muted cry, clinging to Dom as if his life depended on it and shuddering as wave after wave rushed through him.

Dom thrust against him once, twice, more before his whole body tensed and Henry felt his dick pulse as Dom followed him over the edge.

"Wow," Henry murmured, not meaning to say it out loud, but whatever.

Dom's muffled laughter made his body shake, and Henry winced as his now sensitive and sticky cock rubbed against Dom's.

Dom's laughter stopped so abruptly, Henry's started.

"*Stop*," Dom urged, amusement clear in his voice. "Or you'll start me off again, and I can't take it. I need to get out of these fucking boxers and in the shower."

"Me too. I can't believe you made me come in my pants."

Dom started to chuckle again and Henry groaned, pushing at Dom's chest until he rolled to the side.

"Right." Henry finally managed, wiping at his eyes. "Shower."

Dom sat up grimacing, and Henry grinned at the look on his face. But he did exactly the same when he went to stand up.

"Ugh." Taking great care not to smear jizz all down himself, Henry peeled off his underwear and threw them in the direction of the overnight bag he'd taken to bringing with him when he stopped at Dom's villa.

Henry stood stark naked in the middle of the room, watching Dom try and get his wet boxers off and laughing at the look on his face. "Not worth the mess?" Henry asked, wondering if he should feel more self-conscious than he did.

Dom's head whipped up and he fixed Henry with such a heated look, Henry wondered if they were about to go for round two. "Definitely worth it."

Dom's words set off a warm glow inside him, and Henry felt it creep up from his belly, suffusing his chest with a swell of . . . well, whatever it was it had no business being there.

Dom's talking about getting off. Nothing more.

Henry shook his head a little to clear it, but he had no chance of hiding his flush, so he didn't bother trying. Instead, he walked over to Dom, took his hand, and led him into the shower. He didn't speak, not trusting himself to keep his feelings to himself. Knowing his luck, he'd blurt out something along the lines of, *I really want to see you after we leave here.*

Which as he said it in his head, didn't sound like a bad thing. Did it?

It's not what we agreed to.

A holiday fling. That's all.

We're both coming out of failed relationships, he repeated in his head. *Nothing good comes from dating your rebound fuck.*

Describing Dom as that tasted wrong, but that's exactly what he was. Wasn't it?

"Hey, you okay?" Dom stood in front of him, as naked as Henry, and cupped his jaw with both hands.

Henry grumbled under his breath, annoyed with himself for wasting precious time stuck in his own head.

Enjoy your last full day.

Think about all that shit tomorrow.

Yeah. That was a much better plan.

Sliding his hands around Dom's waist, he pulled him close and smiled. "Just thinking about the walkway thing."

Dom kissed the tip of his nose before stepping back, reaching for Henry's hand. "Don't worry. I'll look after you."

"I know you will." And he meant it. Whether it made sense or not, Henry trusted Dom.

"Good." Dom turned the shower on and tugged Henry closer. "Now, come shower with me and we can decide what to do on our last day." He grinned, not seeming bothered at all, and Henry's heart dropped like a stone.

Okay, then. That's fine.

Dom turned to get in under the spray and Henry took a moment to admire his naked form with a wistful sigh.

Better make the most of him while I can.

CHAPTER 7

Dom took Henry for pancakes Thursday night. They'd spent the morning in the sauna and the afternoon playing pool, and despite eating a big lunch, Dom fancied something a little different for tea.

"Pancakes?" Henry scrunched up his nose as they approached the restaurant. "For dinner?" He looked so unconvinced, it was comical.

Dom laughed. He found he did that a lot with Henry. "Christ, I'm not trying to poison you, I promise. And they don't just do sweet ones."

He tugged Henry over to the menu displayed out front.

"Oh." Henry peered at the various options, then shot Dom a sheepish look. "Sorry for doubting you."

"They sound good, right?"

"They do."

Dom felt more than a little smug, pleased that Henry had changed his mind. This particular restaurant was one of his favourites.

"I can't decide to go for savoury or sweet, though. They all look pretty good."

It was on the tip of Dom's tongue to suggest they come back another time, but then he remembered they were almost out of that. The thought was a sobering one and something he didn't want to dwell on.

At the start of the week, six days of no-strings fun had seemed like a great idea, but he hadn't bargained for how well they got on together.

Of course being on holiday, away from their real lives, obviously had an impact too. He'd never have seen this much of Henry if they'd met anywhere other than here.

But they had met, and Dom wasn't sure how he felt about leaving here and never seeing him again.

That's bollocks, and you know it.

Yeah he did know it. The idea of never seeing Henry again wasn't a pleasant one. But they had each other's numbers. It wasn't like they had no way to contact one another.

But would they want to when they were back at home?

Dom couldn't answer that one, so he pushed it away to consider later. For the next twenty-four hours, he had Henry to himself. He refused to waste that time worrying about something that might end up being a non-issue.

"Are we going in?" Henry gestured to the door where a family of four had just disappeared inside. "After looking at the menu, I'm starving."

"Yes, sorry, come on."

They ate way too much, as Dom knew they would. He never managed to resist getting both a savoury and sweet pancake, even though every time he felt comatose afterwards.

They decided to take a walk to work some of it off. Bundled up in coats, hats, and gloves against the elements, Dom steered them towards the wooden walkway down to the lake. "Come on, the firework display should be starting—"

A loud bang tore through the air, and they looked up to see a shower of fireworks above the treetops.

"Now?" Henry finished for him, grinning.

"Apparently so."

They walked quickly, catching the last twenty minutes of the display. Dom bought them both a mulled cider, and they found the perfect spot to drink and watch.

As bright colours lit up the sky, Henry leant into him, his weight solid and right. Dom had the urge to wrap an arm around him and pull him close. Something stopped him, though, and he couldn't decide if it was because they were surrounded by people or because he was trying to remind himself that Henry wasn't actually his boyfriend.

"Why did you and Sam break up?" Henry asked, breaking into Dom's thoughts and taking him by surprise.

He hadn't been expecting that question at all. "Err . . ."

"Sorry, that's probably none of my business. I was just thinking that you know all about why me and Kyle split, and honestly, I'm just being nosy." He laughed and shook his head. "Forget I asked."

But he was right, Dom did know why Henry had split with his boyfriend. Granted, so did a lot of people after his public declaration at the start of the holiday. And wow, didn't that feel like a lifetime ago. "It's nothing as exciting as your story."

Henry snorted. "Tragic, you mean. When it's not a three-way, there's nothing exciting about seeing your boyfriend's cock in another man's arse."

A shocked gasp from behind them had Dom choking on his cider, and Henry quickly turned round to apologise to whoever was unfortunate enough to be behind them.

"Again?" Dom muttered, trying not to laugh.

Henry scowled at him. "What can I say? I have comedic timing." He gestured with his hand for Dom to continue with his tale. "You were saying?"

"Right. Well, it seems to be a pattern with me. I wanted to settle down, maybe get married at some point, I don't know, but I wanted an exclusive relationship and Sam didn't." He shrugged, ignoring the spot inside him that still hurt to talk about it.

What is it with me?

Henry was quiet for a moment and Dom wondered what Henry's thoughts on relationships were.

Probably another reason you should think seriously about contacting Henry after you leave here.

Dom couldn't deny he was still smarting from his and Sam's breakup, and he had no desire for a repeat. No, the next person he got involved with, he'd communicate what he was looking for from the start. If that scared them away, then so be it. It was far worse finding out later, when you were already invested, that the pair of you wanted different things. He'd made that mistake too often.

He nudged Henry's shoulder. "It was no one's fault. I'm not the injured party or anything. We started out casual and didn't communicate properly. By the time we did and discovered we had different needs from our relationship, we were in too deep for it not to hurt." He blew out a breath and glanced up at the night sky, the fireworks coming to the end of their display.

"It was hard, but we're still friends. Albeit tentative ones at the minute, but we'll get there."

"That's nice." Henry said eventually.

"Nice?" Dom asked, eyebrows raised.

"That you can still be friends, after everything." He said quickly. "Not nice that you broke up. Obviously."

"Obviously." Dom laughed softly when Henry elbowed him. "And Sam's a great bloke. I don't want to lose him from my life completely. We were friends first."

Dom finished the rest of his cider and threw his cup in the bin, before facing Henry again. "What about you?"

Henry snorted. "Yeah, there's absolutely no chance I want to remain Kyle's friend."

Dom smiled but rolled his eyes. "That's not what I meant.

Before you found him—" He glanced around them, then lowered his voice. "—fucking his neighbour. Were the two of you serious?"

Henry took a moment to think about it. "No. I don't think we were ever going to last, looking back."

"Oh? Why's that?" Dom's heart stuttered, breath catching as he waited for Henry to elaborate. He didn't know why Henry's answer mattered to him so much—they weren't *together* together —but it did.

Henry sighed. "I think much like your situation. We had different ideas of what our relationship should be." He snorted. "Clearly, judging from the way it ended. But that aside, I reckon me and Kyle weren't in the same place in our lives. And it showed."

What place are you at? Dom was desperate to ask, the question on the tip of his tongue, but if the answer wasn't one he wanted to hear, it would no doubt put a damper on the rest of their time together.

Or maybe add some much-needed perspective?

Either way, the moment passed, and Henry stood, tossing his empty cup in a nearby bin. "Shall we head back?" He shivered and rubbed his hands together. "I don't know about you, but I'm freezing now that the cider's worn off."

Dom nodded, trying to shake the tinge of disappointment threatening to creep in. "Yeah, let's go."

They fell into step with the rest of the crowd heading out now the fireworks were over, a slow progression with sleepy toddlers, and children in pushchairs.

Henry reached for his hand, and despite his reservations brought on by their earlier talk, Dom clasped their fingers together. He'd packed all his things earlier that afternoon, since they planned to stay in Henry's villa tonight. All he had to do was go fetch his car in the morning and load it up.

They didn't talk much on the way back. The silence was a

comfortable one, but it let Dom's mind drift to places he'd rather it wouldn't.

What had Henry meant by that? What did he see when he thought of the future? He was only six years younger than Dom, but he'd only just finished uni. Did he still have that young, care-free mindset? As much as Dom wanted to pursue this thing between them and find out if it could go anywhere once they got home, he wasn't sure he trusted his own judgement anymore.

Yes, Henry was lovely, fun, and unpredictable in a way that kept Dom on his toes. All things he wanted in a partner. But uncertainty about what he wanted for his future definitely wasn't. If that was Henry, then it was far better to enjoy what they were doing now, then end it before either of them got in any deeper.

You already like him a whole lot more than a no-strings arrangement should warrant.

Which was true. Dom always struggled separating sex from emotions. But that was on him. It didn't mean Henry felt the same. And he couldn't ask that question without implying that he wanted to see him again.

And while Dom knew he did, he wasn't so sure that he should.

Henry came to an abrupt stop, and Dom realised with a start that they were back at his villa. He'd managed to walk the whole way home lost in his head.

What great fucking company you are.

Henry shot him a tentative smile. "All right?"

And you're ruining your last night together. Awesome.

Regardless of what came next for them, Dom had plans for tonight. Ones that included getting naked and sweaty, not being all awkward with each other outside Henry's door.

"Sorry for spacing out." He pulled Henry in by his coat and kissed him, trying to convey everything he felt with the soft press of lips and the slide of his tongue as Henry opened up for him. "I was thinking."

"About?" Henry asked as he slipped out of Dom's hold to unlock the door.

No way was Dom about to tell him everything that had run through his head on their walk back, so he settled on the last part. "What I want to do to you once we get inside." The biting wind chose that moment to pick up speed and swirl around them, making them both shudder with cold. "Assuming I can thaw my dick enough to actually use it," he muttered, hustling Henry inside once he got the door open.

Henry's loud laughter filled the small hallway as they hurried to take their coats and boots off, but once inside the living area, the heat hit them and they sighed in unison.

A hand landed on Dom's crotch, palming his very interested cock, and Henry sniggered. "I don't think we'll have a problem."

They shed the rest of their clothes on the way to Henry's bedroom, laughing again as Henry fell over taking off his jeans and landed in a heap on the bed. But when Dom climbed under the covers to join him a few moments later, their laughter died away as the reality hit home.

This was their last night together.

Here.

In a place where real life didn't matter; only they did.

Tomorrow everything would be different, and they'd go their separate ways. Dom didn't want to think about it any longer, so he inched closer, sliding a thigh between Henry's legs and kissing him like it was the last time he'd get to do it.

Because in all likelihood, it would be.

Henry moaned into it, hands sliding around Dom's waist and manoeuvring them both until Dom lay on top of him. They kissed for a long time, holding onto each so tight it was almost painful, their hips rocking together in a slow, sensuous rhythm that set Dom's blood on fire.

Sweat slicked their skin, the bed covers pushed half onto the floor as the heat between them built.

"Want you," Henry murmured, voice muffled where he pressed kiss after kiss against Dom's throat. "Now." He pointed in the general direction of his washbag and Dom got the hint, leaning over to get a condom and lube out of it.

Placing them on the bed next to them, Dom took a moment to compose himself. Propped up on his elbows, he looked down at Henry and his breath caught. With his hair wild and splayed over the pillow, eyes dark and full of the heat Dom felt raging inside him, Henry was the epitome of hot as fuck.

Dom wanted to fuck him so badly, but at the same time he didn't want it to be over.

"All right?" Henry's slight frown had Dom rushing to reassure him.

"Yeah." He ducked his head and kissed him, the soft brush of lips Dom had intended soon morphing into something deeper and way more intense that had them both moaning. He broke away with a soft chuckle. "I was trying to make this last."

Understanding dawned in Henry eyes, and Dom didn't want to think about what came after. He wanted to enjoy this and block everything else out.

Just for a little while.

As Henry slid his hands down Dom's back and grabbed his arse, bringing their hips together again, Dom shot him a grin he didn't entirely feel. "You're not helping."

Henry smirked. "You sure about that?" He rolled his hips, and Dom groaned at the pressure of Henry's cock alongside his own. "Your dick seems to be happy enough with my efforts."

Dom laughed, his smile genuine this time, and pushed himself up onto his knees.

Henry handed him the condom and watched, tongue poking out to lick his bottom lip as Dom ripped open the packet and slowly rolled it down his length. "Fuck," he whispered, gaze darting up to meet Dom's.

"This okay?" Dom asked, taking the bottle of lube and squirting a generous amount on his fingers.

Henry nodded, and spread his legs wide, bringing his knees up to his chest.

Dom forced himself to take his time, working Henry open with careful fingers until he was a writhing, moaning mess, fists clenched so tightly in the bottom sheet his knuckles turned white.

"Enough," he finally hissed, lifting his head to glare at Dom. "Any more prep and I won't even notice you getting in there."

Dom's laughter filled the room, and he sat back giving his aching cock a slow stroke.

Any smart comeback died on his lips as Henry's eyes darkened. He reached for Dom's other hand and said, "I want you to fuck me so good I feel it for days."

When we're no longer together.

Pushing that thought from his mind, Dom shuffled forward and lined himself up before meeting Henry's gaze again. "I can do that."

As he slowly pushed inside him, everything else melted away apart from Henry wrapped around him, tight, despite his grumbling about *too much lube.* Dom grit his teeth as he bottomed out, holding himself still to give them both a second to adjust.

With his usual lack of patience, Henry urged him to move after a few moments. "I'm fine," he whispered, legs wrapping around Dom's back. "Fuck me."

It was the easiest command he'd ever had to follow.

Sliding into Henry's tight heat again and again felt so right, as though they'd done this dance forever. Their bodies moved in synch, Henry meeting each thrust of Dom's hips with his head thrown back, bottom lip caught between his teeth, and a look of such abandon on his face it took everything Dom had not to come at the sight.

But as lovely as that was, he wanted to see Henry's eyes,

needed to feel that connection one more time. "Henry?" he said, voice rough as pleasure lit his veins making words hard to process. "Look at me."

Henry's eyes opened and he slowly focused on Dom, a range of emotions flickering across his face. "Close," he said, sounding as raw as Dom.

Good to know it's not just me.

Grabbing onto Henry's thighs, Dom pushed them up and back and fucked Henry for all he was worth, slamming into him again and again until he was barely hanging on. "Henry...*fuck.*"

Henry shoved his hand between them and grabbed his cock. A few strokes were all it took before he came, a low groan falling from his lips as he shuddered through it.

Dom thrust into him, the sight of his come-covered stomach enough to tip him over the edge, and he clutched Henry tight as his orgasm hit.

They clung to each other, harsh breaths the only sound as they slowly came down.

Dom stayed like that as long as he could, wrapped up in Henry's embrace until he was forced to deal with the condom and clean them both up a bit.

Once back under the quilt, he drew Henry towards him, and cuddled him close.

Neither of them was leaving right away in the morning. They had the walkway and the zipwire still to do in the afternoon, but as Henry leant in and gave him a soft kiss goodnight, it felt like their goodbye all the same.

CHANGEOVER DAYS WERE ALWAYS CHAOTIC, and that Friday was no exception. Having to be out by ten, Dom left Henry's villa just after eight with a quick kiss goodbye and a promise to meet him outside the entrance at the main dome area.

It felt like déjà vu as Dom walked up the path with everyone else leaving that day and saw Henry waiting for him. Who knew that his random act of kindness would lead to this?

Taking pity on a bemused-looking Henry a week ago had been one of the best decisions he'd ever made.

Regardless of what happened after they left.

And Dom fully believed that. He may or may not see Henry again, but the last seven days had been wonderful, and he wouldn't change that for anything.

"Hey," he said as he reached him. "Want to walk down to the lake and get a coffee?"

Henry smirked. "I feel like we've done this before."

"I was just thinking the same thing."

They stood there smiling at each other like idiots until Dom shook his head and gently steered Henry towards the path. "We've got some time to kill before our walkway slot."

Henry winced. "How could I forget."

"Hey," Dom said, taking Henry's hand. "You don't have to do it, you know."

"I do." Henry grimaced, looking up at the tall trees surrounding the lake. Then he gave a self-deprecating laugh. "I'm just a bit scared. Ridiculous, right? Kids as young as eight do it, for fuck's sake."

Guilt seeped in as Dom wondered if this was his fault. He'd banged on about the fucking zipwire enough times over the past few days. Had Henry felt pressured to do something that obviously terrified him? "Look, why don't we try the sauna instead. I'm sure they've got a couple of spaces for this afternoon."

Henry stared at him, mouth open. "But we've paid. Well, you have. I still owe you for that."

Dom waved him away. "I'm not bothered about the money. I don't want to do something that clearly terrifies you when we could be relaxing in a nice hot sauna without a zipwire in sight." Yeah, he'd been looking forward to it, but not if it meant

Henry was going to be scared shitless. There was no fun in that.

Henry's smile started off small as he focused on his boots, gradually getting bigger until he was beaming by the time he met Dom's gaze. "Thank you."

Dom smiled in return, happy to see the tension in Henry's eyes ease a little. "You're welcome. Now let's go see if we can book that sauna." He stopped and frowned. "Then we'll have to nip back to the car park because I left my swimming—"

"We won't."

"Erm . . ." Dom held out his hands, showing Henry he had nothing on him but his keys, wallet, and phone. "We will if we want to go in the sauna. Pretty sure nakedness is frowned upon."

Henry laughed loudly, scaring a few nearby birds into flight. "We don't need swimming gear because we're still doing the high-as-fuck walkway thing."

Now Dom was totally confused. "But I thought . . . ?"

Henry stepped closer, linking his fingers with Dom's. "Thank you for thinking of me enough to give up something I know you've been looking forward to all week. But I'm going to do it. With you."

"Aren't you scared?"

"Terrified." He squeezed Dom's fingers. "But also weirdly excited. Does that make sense?"

Dom shook his head. "In no way."

Henry laughed, head thrown back, and Dom was captivated by the sight. The light stubble along his jawline, the bob of his Adam's apple as he swallowed, and the light in his eyes as he looked back at Dom.

He wanted to kiss him so badly in that moment, it took all his willpower not to. Only the fact they were surrounded by people kept him rooted in place. "Are you sure about this?"

"No, but I know I'll regret it if I don't give it a go."

They started walking again, and Dom felt the need to point

something out. As they neared the start of the walkway course, he gestured to where the first obstacle was visible through the trees. "There's about eight people per session. All attached by a harness and rope to the overhead rope that runs the entire course. Once you're up there"—he pointed up in the trees—"it's not all that easy to get down if you change your mind. They'd do it, obviously," he added when Henry's eyes widened comically. "But far better to not go up at all if you're unsure."

Henry raised an eyebrow. "Are you trying to talk me out of it?"

"No." *I'm trying to stop you having a freak-out in the middle of the trees.* Dom had no idea exactly how bad Henry's fear of heights was, but he knew it felt a lot higher than it actually was when trying to walk over swaying log bridges with nothing but a rope overhead.

"Okay then. It's settled. We're doing it. Now let's go get some coffee in the warmth so my fingers aren't blocks of ice when I need to hold onto things."

WHAT THE FUCK had I been thinking?

Side-walking up the first log at the start of the walkway had been bad enough. Henry flushed at the memory of him wobbling like jelly on a plate.

But this?

He stood on the first platform, back plastered to the large tree trunk, heart racing as he watched the two kids—they couldn't have been older than nine or ten—skip over the swaying planks of the bridge to their dad at the other end. They whooped in delight, and Henry groaned because that meant only one thing.

It's my turn.

Dom smiled encouragingly. "Take it one step at a time."

"Mm-hmm." Henry grabbed the rope rails on either side and took a tentative first step.

The whole bridge began to sway gently, and Henry grit his teeth against the urge to turn back and beg someone to get him down.

For fuck's sake, Henry. You can do this.

He took another step, to the delight of Dom calling encouragement from behind him. It made him smile, at least.

"One at a time, keep going," Dom shouted, as Henry gingerly made his way across. As he stepped off onto the solid platform at the other end, he hugged the tree trunk like a long-lost friend and let out a huge sigh of relief.

"Woo-hoo!" Dom yelled, making him laugh this time. "That's it."

Henry felt ridiculously pleased with himself, even if it was one of the easier pieces they'd have to cross, because he'd fucking done it, and in his mind that was huge.

Dom made it look easy, of course, taking half the time Henry did to make his way across. His huge smile was infectious, though, and despite his thudding pulse, Henry found himself grinning back.

Of course, that vanished as soon as he saw the next fucking thing they had to cross.

But he made it.

And that's how it went for the next four bridge-type things they had to traverse. Heart-racing terror as he made his way across, then sheer relief when he got to the other side.

It was exhausting.

Sweat trickled down his spine and Henry had to wipe his forehead a couple of times, but he didn't care, because Dom never let up in his encouragement or his delight when Henry made it across. His never-ending enthusiasm and utter belief that Henry could do it was the main thing that kept him going.

Until they came to the jump.

It wasn't even a big jump.

Probably just longer than a stride gap between two platforms, but to Henry it felt like a huge abyss. His mouth went dry, sweat coating his upper lip, as he tried and failed not to look down.

"Fuck," he muttered, clinging to the metal handholds on the tree. "I can't."

Dom shuffled up behind him, not quite touching, but Henry felt him everywhere, nonetheless. "You can, Henry." He leant in close to place a quick, chaste kiss on the back of Henry's neck. "You've done so fucking well so far. You can do this too."

Henry shook his head. "I can't. I know it's ridiculous, but my legs won't fucking move."

Dom tsked gently. "It's not ridiculous. And I know you're scared, but I also know that you *can* do it." He took Henry's hand in his, obviously not caring if anyone saw them, and held tight. "It's one step, just a little wider than if you were walking. Breathe, Henry."

Henry did as he was told.

He took several long deep breaths in and out, Dom's body a comforting presence that did enough to calm his racing heart so Henry could think.

Taking a good long look at the gap, Henry bit his lip, steeling himself.

I can fucking do this.

Before he could psych himself out of it, he let go of Dom's hand and leapt across to the other platform. His heart hammered against his chest, and he clung like a limpet to the handholds on the tree, but he was across.

Fuck me.

He grinned so wide his cheeks hurt, and Dom's cheer made him laugh way too loudly. Adrenaline coursed through him, and in that one moment, Henry felt like he could do anything.

Of course, that didn't last, and it was rinse and repeat as they worked their way through the rest of the course. By the time they climbed the netting up to the zipwire platform, Henry was knackered.

He felt like he'd run a marathon rather than spent forty minutes in the trees.

That wasn't the only thing.

While he'd been aware subconsciously that they'd been steadily getting higher and higher, stepping out onto the zipwire platform took his breath away.

It. Was. So. Fucking. High.

Rationally he'd known it would be if they were going to get the sort of traction they needed, but *Christ*.

"All right?" Dom asked, climbing up behind him.

Henry didn't know whether to lie or be brutally honest.

"No." Honesty it was. He darted an anxious look at Dom. "It's a tad higher than I was expecting."

Dom huffed out a laugh at his understatement. "It is." He tugged on the safety rope and then his harness. "But you're perfectly safe. Watch." He gently turned Henry around to watch the two kids in front of them waiting at the edge of the platform.

Two of the instructors, also harnessed and attached by safety ropes, were talking to them, telling them what to do when they reached the bottom. Henry only half-listened, heart beating a heavy drum inside his head.

On a count of three, both kids sat back into their harnesses, then stepped off the platform, squealing with delight as they careered down the zipwire. Henry watched them the whole way until they came to a swinging halt at the other end.

He swallowed down the huge lump in his throat.

Right. There is no way I've gone through the last forty minutes just to fail at the last hurdle. Come on, Henry.

As the guy ushered them both forward, Dom whispered. "This is the best bit, trust me." He smiled encouragingly, and Henry felt a little of his panic chip away.

He did trust Dom.

Not that he wasn't still petrified, because he was, but having Dom there beside him, full of belief in him, gave Henry that little extra courage he needed.

Enough to step off that fucking platform into mid-air.

The instructor went through his spiel. "Sit back in your harness. Slowly step off the platform." Henry listened intently to all of it, nodding when asked if he was ready to go.

It felt a bit like an out of body experience. Like it was someone else shuffling towards the edge and stepping off into *absolutely fucking nothing.*

Oh my god!

Henry's heart was in his throat for that split second before the zipwire took his weight, and then he was whizzing downwards, the wind whipping his face, and a laugh bubbled out of him.

This is amazing!

He'd never felt anything like it, and he grinned wildly, finally taking the opportunity to look down and around him as he flew over the lake. He could see everything: the trees stretching out in all directions, the top of the dome in the distance.

And Dom next to him, legs indeed flailing around like everybody else.

Perfect.

The whole thing was awesome, but over way too quickly, and Henry came to a jarring halt at the bottom.

Grabbing the rope tossed to him by another instructor, he hauled himself up the netting and onto the very last platform.

His legs shook and his pulse was still way too fast, but Henry had never felt more alive. He climbed down to the ground to meet Dom, unable to stop smiling, even though he probably looked like a crazed idiot.

And totally forgetting where they were, Henry wrapped his arms around Dom and hugged him tight. "Oh my god, that was amazing. Thank you so fucking much."

Dom's laughter, warm and rich, sounded in his ear, and Henry buried his face in Dom's neck, letting it wash over him. "Don't thank me, that was all you. You were awesome up there."

Henry snorted. "Yeah, right. I was petrified. There were ten-year-old kids way braver than me."

Dom pulled back to look at him, and the intensity of his gaze stunned Henry silent. He didn't remember anyone ever looking at him like that before. "You were terrified, but you still did it. I'm in awe." Dom kissed him quickly, a fleeting touch of lips, then stepped back looking sheepish. "I want to do inappropriate things to you right now."

The flutter in his stomach wasn't from fright this time.

How am I supposed to let you go when you do things like this?

Was this still a no-strings arrangement? Henry felt off-kilter suddenly, but that might've been the adrenaline still flooding his system. Who knew?

"Let's go back to my vi—"

Fuck.

They had no villas anymore.

The unfinished sentence hung between them and Henry stood there, unsure of what to do. "Do you fancy another coffee?" Lame, but it was the only thing he could think to offer.

Dom's sigh said it all, and Henry's stomach dropped, the fluttery feeling all but stamped out with Dom's next words. "I'm sorry, I can't. I need to leave soon."

"Soon?" Henry tried to sound nonchalant but knew he'd failed to pull it off.

Dom blew out a breath, the warm air misty in the chill afternoon. "In the next thirty minutes or so. I wish I could stay longer, but . . ." He held out his arms in a slightly helpless gesture. Like it was all out of his hands.

Of course, he had a life to get back to.

They'd both been playing pretend for the last week, Henry reminded himself. None of this was real.

It sure as fuck feels real.

"Well," Henry said, clapping his hands together and plastering a smile on his face. "We better get these back, then." He tugged at his harness, then gestured behind them to the small clearing where all the gear was stored.

Dom studied him, probably wondering why he was so over-the-top cheerful all of a sudden, but Henry couldn't seem to rein it in.

"You ready?" His smile felt forced, wooden, and judging by Dom's expression, he knew it too. But he said nothing, just nodded and gestured for Henry to lead the way.

They walked in silence all the way to the instructor's hut. Handing over their harnesses took only a few minutes, and Henry felt their time together slipping away like sand through his fingers.

But there was nothing he could do to prolong it.

He had work in the morning.

Dom probably had a million things planned for when he got back.

A week was all they'd agreed to and that was over.

Finished.

With a heavy heart, Henry followed Dom to the path, and they began the long walk back to the car park.

CHAPTER 8

"I'm parked over there." Henry pointed to the far-right side of the car park.

Dom offered him a rueful smile and gestured in the opposite direction. "I'm over there."

Of course he was. Henry couldn't seem to catch a fucking break.

"Oh." Henry bit his lip, unsure how to play this.

Do I ask to see him again? Do I just say goodbye and leave it at that?

While Henry had no wish to embarrass himself, he didn't want his fear of rejection to stop them carrying this on if there was even the slightest chance Dom was feeling the same way.

What Henry really wanted to do was pull him in for a kiss goodbye. A proper one, with tongues and arse-grabbing. But the car park had a steady stream of people both leaving and arriving, so a bit of lip action and some casual groping was unfortunately out of the question.

Henry toed at the dried, dead leaves on the ground as he spoke.

"So, um—"

"Right, I'd better—"

Henry's head snapped up and he met Dom's amused gaze. They laughed awkwardly, which struck Henry as a little ironic. He hadn't felt like that with Dom even when they'd met for the very first time, yet here they were after a week in each other's pockets dancing around each other like strangers.

Maybe underneath it all we still are?

"Hey." Dom's softly spoken word brought Henry back to the present. His hand on Henry's made his pulse race and hope flare in his chest. "You have my number." He squeezed Henry's fingers. "Use it."

And then with one last smile, he was gone.

Henry stood rooted to the spot, powerless to do anything other than watch Dom walk away.

Right.

He replayed Dom's words in his head. Torn between a feeling of *yes!* and *what the fuck?*

It hadn't been an outright "no I don't want to see you again, Henry," but neither was it a definite "Let's meet up for a drink next week." He'd left the ball entirely in Henry's court, and Henry wasn't at all sure how he felt about that.

Finally forcing his feet to move, he walked in the direction of his car, mulling over the many possible meanings of Dom's parting words.

I should have asked him.

Henry grumbled at his inability to act all the way back to his car. As he sat drumming his fingers on the steering wheel, he resolved to take Dom at his word.

I do have his number, and I will fucking use it.

Jesus Christ.

"*You have my number. Use it.*" Dom shook his head, rolling his eyes for good measure. He'd sounded like a twat. What had possessed him to say something so . . . so . . . ? Fuck, he couldn't even find the words.

Henry had telegraphed what he wanted loud and clear. Dom couldn't even plead ignorance, it'd been written all over his face.

Henry wanted to see him again.

He might not have said the words, Dom hadn't given him much of a chance.

You ran away.

"Fuck," he hissed under his breath but still managed to startle a couple walking past him. He muttered an apology and immediately thought of Henry.

And that spike of guilt hit him all over again.

Putting all the onus on Henry had been a cowardly thing to do. He was thirty-two years old, for fuck's sake. Surely he'd reach the age where he could have a conversation about whether he wanted to carry on seeing the guy he'd been fucking for the past week.

Fucking?

Dom winced. It had been more than sex, who was he kidding? Would it translate to their normal lives once they had to deal with the mundane shit like work, family, and the fact they lived a good hour apart? Dom had no idea.

And you won't unless you give it a try.

He went back and forth over the idea all the way home. He might have left Henry with a dramatic declaration, but the reality was he had Henry's number too. There was nothing to stop him from making the first move to initiate contact.

And he wanted to see Henry again. He didn't even try to deny it. But where would it lead?

Dom sighed, all the good feelings his week away had brought, now tinged with doubt as he struggled to figure out if what he wanted was also what he needed.

One thing he did know, he needed a beer and to chew someone's ear off.

"So let me get this straight," Nathan said, handing Dom a beer and rolling his eyes at Dom's snort. "You met someone, spent the week together having glorious no-strings sex, you like him, he likes you, yet you don't know whether to see him again." He raised his eyebrows. "Is that the gist of it?"

"Pretty much." Dom took a long pull from his bottle, then pointed it at Nathan. "You make it sound so straightforward when you put it like that."

"That's because it is." Luke, Nathan's partner of five years, walked into the kitchen wearing low-slung pyjama bottoms and nothing else. He leant against the worktop next to Nathan. "You always make things way too complicated."

"Fuck off." Dom smiled to take the sting out of it and took a moment to admire the toned muscles Luke shamelessly showed off. He sighed and ran his fingers through his poor, abused hair. He'd had his hands in it all the way home. "It is complicated."

"Why?" Nathan asked, crossing his arms. Luke did the same and Dom laughed because the pair of them looked like a couple of bouncers about to ask him to leave. His phone chimed with a text before he could comment, and all thoughts left him as he stared at the name displayed on his screen.

Henry.

Dom swallowed, inexplicably nervous all of a sudden.

It's just a text.

Only Henry's name appeared, none of the message. If Dom wanted to read it, he'd have to unlock his phone, and his thumb hovered over it while he weighed up whether to do it now or later.

"Is that him?" Luke asked. When Dom nodded, he darted forward like a cat and snatched up Dom's phone.

"Hey!" he protested as Luke tapped the screen.

"Sorry, but you were taking way too long, and you need an intervention."

"I do not." Dom shot back.

"Aha." Luke grinned in triumph.

"And how do you know my fucking password?"

He gave Dom a pointed look. "It's your birthday. You've used it as your passcode for fucking ever."

Not anymore.

"Stop reading my messages," Dom grumbled, but Luke ignored him and tilted the phone screen for Nathan to read.

Curiosity finally outweighed being pissed off, and Dom sighed. "Fine, what does it say?"

Luke handed the phone back to him. "See for yourself."

Reluctantly, Dom took it and read what was on the screen.

Henry: *So, this is me, using your number :) I've just got home, and I've got to say I miss being on holiday already. Not looking forward to work in the morning. Hope you got back ok. x*

"Huh." Honestly, he was a bit disappointed, which he knew he had no right to be, but he'd been expecting a request to meet up.

Not whatever *that* was.

Dom set his phone down on the counter and glanced up to find Nathan and Luke staring at him. "What?"

"Aren't you going to reply?" Nathan asked.

Dom took another drink of his beer, putting off answering. "I don't know."

Nathan gave in and took a seat next to Dom at the breakfast bar. He nudged his shoulder. "He's testing the water with that text."

"I know."

"If you aren't interested in seeing him again, then tell him."

Dom picked up his phone, then put it down again. "I do want to see him again. I think."

"You think?" Nathan cocked an eyebrow. "Either you like him or you don't. It's not rocket science."

But it wasn't that easy. "I do like him, I just don't know if I see it leading anywhere, and I don't want to go down that path again."

Nathan knew better than anyone about Dom's previous relationship breakdowns. He'd been the one to pick Dom up, dust him off, and tell him to get back out there. More than once.

Dom could tell from the set of his jaw that Nathan was about to do something similar again, so he held up a hand to forestall the lecture. "I know what you're going to say."

"Good, saves me the trouble of repeating myself."

Dom laughed, but it died away quickly. "Maybe it's better to keep it as a holiday fling and leave it at that. I'm still adjusting to breaking up with Sam. I don't think jumping into something new, with someone who lives over an hour away, is the best thing for me at the moment."

Nathan sighed but conceded Dom's point with a nod. "Okay, I get what you're saying." He squeezed Dom's shoulder. "But the timing of these things isn't always perfect. Don't let something good slip through your fingers because you're scared of getting hurt again."

NATHAN'S WORDS stayed with him all night.

It was easy for Nathan to hand out advice. He was happily shacked up with the love of his life, had known Luke was *it* for him about a week after they met.

It wasn't like that for Dom. Not anymore. He didn't trust himself to make the smart decisions where his love life was concerned.

It wasn't until he lay in bed that night that he finally replied to Henry.

Dom: *Hey, sorry for not replying sooner. Was at a friend's. I got back ok, thanks. And yeah, I'm not looking forward to work either.*

He umm'd and ahh'd over adding a kiss for so long he accidentally hit Send by mistake.

Rereading the text made him wince. *Jesus.* He'd be amazed if Henry ever texted him again. And that was a sobering thought, because for all Dom's doubts about exploring a relationship with him, he didn't want Henry to stop messaging him.

He thought about sending a follow-up text, opened the app, then closed it again.

Nah, better to wait until I can get my head sorted.

HENRY SAT at his kitchen table and stared at Dom's text message for about the twentieth time and yet still had no idea where he stood.

Where *they* stood.

They'd been texting back and forth for a week now. Just one text a day to start with, gradually building up to three, sometimes four.

While Henry enjoyed what they were doing—he lunged for his phone every time it pinged with a text—he still felt in some sort of limbo. Granted, his last message to Dom hadn't been anything exciting, but he'd started the conversation and he'd hoped Dom might give him something to work with.

He read through their message thread again.

Henry: *Looking forward to the weekend, only working Saturday morning, so get the rest of it off. What're you up to this weekend?*

Dom: *Nothing much, work probably. It's super busy at the minute.*

He'd hoped Dom might take the hint that he was free and maybe, oh I don't know, ask to meet up.

Nope.

Henry got the feeling Dom purposely ignored it.

"Oh my god, reply already." Jason wandered into the kitchen in his pyjamas, yawning. Out of the three people that Henry shared a house with, Jason was probably his closest friend.

The only one he'd confided in about Dom.

Jason sat down next to him and bumped their shoulders. "Staring at it won't make it say anything different."

"I know that," Henry grumbled. With a heavy sigh, he set his phone on the table and picked up his mug of tea. "I just don't know what to say."

"Well . . ." Jason reached over and snagged a piece of Henry's toast.

Henry glared at him, but he wasn't going to eat it anyway, so he let it slide.

"Well, what?"

"You could ask him if he wants to see you again." Jason munched on his stolen toast, giving Henry's phone a pointed look.

"I don't know." Henry thought about their awkward goodbye in the car park. "I get the feeling he's not all that sure about keeping in contact."

"He did reply to your text, though, and you might as well ask him outright instead of sitting here torturing yourself." Jason glanced at Henry's phone again and frowned. "And not to alarm you, but shouldn't you be leaving soon?"

Henry looked at the time and cursed. "Why didn't you tell me it was that late? *Fuck.*"

Downing a last mouthful of tea, Henry chucked his pots in the sink and then raced up the stairs to clean his teeth and get changed into his uniform.

A uniform that now consisted of a vary garish Christmas jumper with reindeers and bells.

He made it to work with a minute to spare. But rushing to get ready had meant he still hadn't replied to Dom's text. Not that it needed a reply, but Henry liked to keep their conversations going.

Shoving his wallet, keys, and phone into his locker, Henry glanced out the window of the staffroom. Not seeing any of his immediate supervisors, he typed out a quick text to Dom.

Henry: *Work's shit already and I've only just got here. Hope your day is going better than mine.*

He pressed Send before he could rethink it, placed his phone in his locker with everything else, and closed the door.

Out of sight, hopefully out of mind.

Wrong.

So very wrong.

Henry's day dragged. Despite the Christmas music playing round the clock and the decorations—which he had to admit were quite tasteful—Henry felt far from festive.

If he had to look at another box of Heroes or Quality Street, he might hurl, and why was all the chocolate suddenly orange flavoured?

I don't get it.

He'd also had enough of dealing with customers. Throwing a bag for life at him wasn't the way to get him to pack the fucking shopping. A simple please and thank you would work a whole lot better.

When his break finally rolled around, Henry almost fell onto one of the stools in the staffroom with an energy drink and a protein bar for company. Snatching his phone from his locker, Henry's pulse picked up at the sight of Dom's name on his screen.

Dom: *Well, I've dropped a box full of glass Christmas ornaments, burnt my tongue on a cup of coffee, and slipped over while moving Christmas trees so now my arse is covered in mud. Can you top that?*

Henry laughed loudly before remembering where he was and covering his mouth. The last thing he wanted was his nosey colleagues wandering in with questions.

Henry: *I'm wearing this . . .*

He snapped a selfie of his Christmas jumper, making sure to get the reindeer in all their bell-covered glory.

Henry: *I think I win.*

It took a few minutes for Dom to reply, and Henry watched the three little dots as if they held the answers to everything.

Dom: *Oh that's bad, but pretty sure I have you beat . . .*

A photo appeared as Henry was taking a drink and he almost choked trying to swallow it down.

Fuck me.

He drank in the photo of Dom, dressed in a bright red Santa jumper, with a pair of red sparkly antlers perched on his head.

Henry: *Very festive.*

And hot, he wanted to add, but they seemed to have moved into this weird friend-zone since they'd returned to real life, and Henry wasn't sure how to get out of it.

If he brought up their week together, would Dom go radio silent? Or was Dom staring at his phone like Henry was, waiting for him to mention it first.

Christ. Why was this so hard?

He ran a hand through his hair, watching the three little dots on his phone and waiting impatiently for Dom's reply.

Dom: *It's my punishment for breaking my mum's ornaments.*

Henry grinned.

Henry: *I think you got off lightly.*

Dom: *Me too. She made my brothers sing Christmas carols when they broke her light-up Santas. By the front of the café as people were coming in.*

Henry laughed again and hurried to reply.

Henry: *She sounds fearsome.*

Dom: *Nah, she's five foot four and soft as a brush. They just wanted to get in her good books to get free cakes.*

Henry: *Is that why you're wearing antlers?*

Dom: *Busted.*

Okay. So maybe Dom wanted to try and be friends first before meeting up again? Henry could do that. Play the texting game while they found their feet back in their normal lives.

He only had a few more minutes left on his break, so he hurriedly texted back.

Henry: *Fair enough. I'd wear antlers for free cake.*

Henry: *Got to get back to work now, chat later.*

He hesitated before hitting Send, finger hovering over the x key, but didn't press it. Dom hadn't added a kiss to any of his messages after all. With a sigh, he sent it off, and returned his phone to his locker.

Only another three hours to go.

HENRY WENT STRAIGHT from work to Ella's. She'd offered to cook him tea in exchange for details about his holiday.

Since he'd probably tell her everything anyway, Henry figured he was getting the better deal. He checked his phone as he parked on her drive. Dom hadn't sent him anything since their conversation earlier. Not that Henry had sent anything either, but then Henry had worked until eight o'clock in the end. Surely Dom finished earlier than that?

Henry frowned. He actually had no idea what time garden centres stayed open till.

But then Dom didn't have to message him. It wasn't as though they were together or anything. Tired of looking for hidden meanings in everything, and just fucking tired in general, Henry got out of his car and shoved his phone in his back pocket.

Ella would kill him if he sat staring at it all night.

"Henry!" She greeted him at the door with a hug and a smile.

He sank into her arms, closing his eyes and hugging her back for a long moment. As annoying as his sister could be, she was also his rock when his life invariably turned to shit.

She gave him a curious look when they separated. "You okay?"

"Yeah, just tired." He ushered her back into the house when she seemed about to interrogate him. "Something smells good." Praising her culinary skills was a sure-fire way to distract.

Always worked like a charm.

"Mum finally got round to sending me her lasagne recipe, so I thought you could be my guinea pig."

"You've only got one brother, remember."

Rolling her eyes, she turned and headed into the kitchen, Henry hot on her heels.

Distraction techniques aside, it did smell amazing, and he was starving.

"I bought the garlic bread," she said, fetching a tray out of the oven. "Couldn't be arsed faffing about with that."

"But lasagne was so much easier?" He shook his head at her and took a seat at her breakfast bar, watching her dish up their tea.

"No, but I'd had enough cooking by then." She shoved a plate in front of him. "Shut up and eat. Then you can tell me all about your week of sex and debauchery."

Henry choked on his drink for the second time that day.

Of course she waited until he'd taken a sip of water.

Before he could retaliate, his phone buzzed in his pocket with a text message, and he almost knocked his glass over in his haste to read it.

It wasn't from Dom, and he let out a small huff of disappointment, setting his phone on the worktop next to him.

Ella watched it all with a raised eyebrow.

Henry picked up his cutlery, knowing she was going to be

asking all sorts of questions now. "After we've eaten," he muttered.

But eating in silence made him far more uneasy than having Ella grilling him about it all, so ten minutes into their meal, he pulled up his recent message thread with Dom and shoved his phone at her.

"He friend-zoned me and I'm not sure how to get out of it."

Ella skimmed through their texts, brow getting more furrowed as she read. "Oh," she said, setting his phone back down.

"Oh? What does that mean?"

"Nothing." She gestured to his phone. "I mean, at least he's replying to your messages."

"But?"

"But considering you just shared a week of torrid sex—"

Henry snorted. "Just say we spent the week together. You're making it sound ridiculous."

She smirked at him. "Was the sex not torrid and debauched, Henry? Is that why you're now his bestie instead of his lover."

"The sex was fine."

"*Fine?*"

He threw his hands in the air. "Oh my god, yes, the sex was hot and awesome and definitely not the reason why he's sending me Christmas jumper pics instead of—" He clamped his lips together.

"Dick pics?" She ventured, laughing. "Is that what you want him to send you?"

"No, of course not."

Maybe? Henry shifted on his stool, ignoring the curl of heat in his belly at the thought of Dom's dick.

"Mm-hmm." Ella stood and cleared their plates away, waving Henry to sit back down when he went to help her. "How did you leave things between you? Did you talk about meeting up again?"

"Not exactly." Henry recounted their awkward moment in the

car park, cringing at his inability to simply tell Dom what he wanted.

She passed him a beer from the fridge and patted his shoulder. "I don't know what to say."

"That'll be a first." Henry suspected it was more like she didn't know what to say without confirming his fear that Dom wasn't interested in seeing him again. At least not in the way they'd seen each other the week before. "You don't have to be diplomatic."

She laughed at him, nudging his shoulder as she took her seat next to him. "Since when have I ever been diplomatic?"

He tipped his beer at her. "Good point."

"It's just, you said the week was great, right?"

"Yep."

"And you like him a lot, and you think he liked you too?"

Henry took a pull of his beer and thought back over everything they'd done together. "I kinda got that feeling, yeah."

"But neither of you mentioned meeting up again when you parted ways?"

"No."

She huffed out a frustrated breath. "See, that's the part I just don't get. If you both liked each other, why the fuck wouldn't you ask to see him again?"

"Hey," Henry protested. "It wasn't just me."

"Yes, I know, but you're the only one here, so . . ." She waved a hand at him.

He set his beer down more forcefully than he intended. "I don't know what to do, El."

"What does your gut tell you?" She reached for his hand and held it tight. "Even if we sometimes don't want to listen, I always think deep down we know."

Henry mulled over her words. "I know we were only together for a week, but it was kind of intense, and I got the feeling it was more than just sex at the end."

"Okay then." She nudged his phone towards him. "Wait for the right moment and ask him if he's interested in meeting up. At least then you'll know where you stand and can either move on or start to get to know him better."

"You make it sound so simple."

"That's because it is." She squeezed his hand again, then stood. "Stop making it more complicated than it needs to be."

Henry thought about texting Dom all the way home.

I could call him.

That would be better than trying to guess the tone of his texts, but Henry shied away from that idea. With a text he could get the words right before hitting Send. If he called, he'd have no do overs, and he knew he got flustered sometimes and things came out wrong.

And Dom hadn't called him either.

Ugh.

Henry yawned as he parked outside his house, no nearer to deciding the best course of action.

His phone chimed as he unlocked his front door, Dom's name on his screen waking the butterflies in his belly.

Dom: *Hey, sorry I didn't reply. Everyone and his dog wanted a Xmas tree today.*

Henry kicked his shoes off, hung up his coat and glanced around their bare hallway. They had no lights, no tree, not even a fucking wreath on the door.

It was already December ninth, but you'd never guess looking at Henry's house.

Jason lay sprawled on the sofa. When Henry walked into the living room, he glanced up. "Hey."

"Hey." Henry gestured to the empty space in the bay window. "Do you think we should get a tree?"

Jason paused the TV show he was watching and grinned.

"Yeah. This place needs fucking cheering up. It's depressing after being surrounded by Christmassy shit all day at work."

"It is." As much as Henry moaned about the decorations at work, it certainly felt Christmassy inside. And coming back home to nothing was depressing. "Next weekend," Henry said, nodding his head decisively. "We'll go get a fucking tree."

Jason grinned up at him. "I like this new you. Very assertive." His expression turned sly. "Must've been all that sex you had last week." His gaze dropped to Henry's phone, still clutched in his hand. "Talking of which . . . ?"

Henry winced. "I haven't asked him about meeting up." He raised a hand, cutting off whatever sage advice Jason was about to bestow on him. "I'm working up to it."

"Okay."

Oh. Henry hadn't expected him to let it go so easily.

He's not Ella, he reminded himself. "Right, I'm off to bed, see you tomorrow."

Jason waved at him, eyes glued to the TV, and Henry left him to it, trudging upstairs to his bedroom.

He waited until he was in bed to reply to Dom's text.

Henry: *That's ok, I was busy too.*

He'd almost told Dom about food retail being one of the worst places to work this time of year, but something stopped him.

Did I tell him where I worked?

They'd talked about so much in that week, Henry couldn't remember if he had or not. He didn't want to remind him of the fact that he had a degree he couldn't get a job with. Not one he wanted, anyway.

Maybe staying friends was for the best. Real-life Henry might be a huge disappointment.

His phone chimed again, startling him.

Dom: *Going to sleep. Knackered.*

Henry stared at the phone for a while before replying. If a

simple text goodnight made his stomach flutter and his pulse race, maybe it was worth taking a little risk?

Henry opened the message app and typed his reply.

Henry: *Night, Dom. Talk to you tomorrow. x*

Biting his lip, his finger hovered over the Send key, but he chickened out and deleted the kiss.

Fuck.

Next time.

Dom replied just as Henry reached to turn his light out.

Dom: *Night, Henry.*

CHAPTER 9

As much as Dom loved all things Christmas, being surrounded by it all day, every day was getting a bit much even for him. Christmas songs played on repeat in the café and in the shop.

Decorations adorned everywhere that the general public were likely to go, and if he had to wrap one more fucking tree, he might scream.

Okay, that was probably an exaggeration, but by the time lunchtime came around he was more than happy to retreat to the blessedly quiet staffroom and put his feet up for half an hour.

Sandwich in one hand, he pulled out his phone with the other. He kept it turned off while working, less tempting that way, so seeing two new messages from Henry came as a pleasant surprise.

The first was a photo of someone's living room, with the caption, "What's wrong with this picture?"

Dom frowned. It looked like a nice, normal room to him. Big sofa, TV, etc.

He scrolled to the next message.

Henry: I'll give you a clue. I took that at my house this morning.

It took Dom a moment to realise what was missing.

Dom: *Do you even know what month it is?*

Dom: *Where's your tree?*

He'd seen Henry admire all the decorations at the holiday park, so he knew he liked them. Why didn't he have any of his own? It was the middle of December. Dom was just about to ask when he saw the tell-tale dots telling him Henry was replying.

They disappeared and reappeared a few times before an actual message came through.

Henry: *We just haven't got round to getting it yet.*

Dom: *We?*

Dom stared at his phone, an uncomfortable feeling growing in his belly. Was he back with his arsehole of an ex? Surely not in the short amount of time since they'd got back.

Unless it was all a lie and Henry hadn't broken up with anyone?

Fuck.

Dom felt a little sick at the thought it had all been an act.

Thank fuck, I didn't—

Henry: *I share a house with three of my mates.*

Oh.

Dom felt ridiculously relieved, then confused.

Dom: *You gave me the impression you lived on your own.*

Not that it mattered either way. Buying a house or renting on your own was fucking expensive. Dom had been lucky he'd bought his from family at a much cheaper price than he'd have otherwise got. But he was curious as to why Henry had never mentioned it when they'd talked about nearly everything else.

Henry's reply took a long while to come, and Dom was about to go back to work when the notification appeared on his phone.

Henry: *I know. I was embarrassed. You have a great job and bought your own house. I can't seem to get the job I want and still share a house with my mates at 26.*

Dom stared at his phone, unsure how to reply, but some things began to slot into place.

Not to be big-headed, but Dom had known Henry liked him, and not just as a holiday fuckbuddy. Dom had his own issues and reasons for not asking to see Henry again, but if he was being honest, he'd fully expected Henry to bring it up.

And the fact that he hasn't is disappointing.

It was.

Hypocritical too, because he'd spent Friday night telling his friends just why seeing Henry again was an epically bad idea, yet it hurt that Henry didn't seem to want to see him either.

Maybe that was why.

It occurred to him, belatedly, that he'd left Henry hanging after he'd admitted to what must have been a huge thing for him. God knew what must be going through his mind at Dom ignoring him.

Bollocks.

Dom: *You've only just finished uni. Might take time to get your dream job. Hang in there. And there's no shame in living with your mates. Housing is expensive these days.*

He wanted to say more to convince Henry that there was no need to be embarrassed, but he didn't want to risk sounding like a patronising arse. He quickly reread the message he'd sent, hoping he hadn't come off like that.

"Dom?"

Dom's head shot up as his mum popped her head around the door. "Hey."

She smiled. "Can you help me move a couple of things in the shop? My back's been playing up today."

As much as he wanted to wait for Henry's reply, Dom turned his phone to silent and shoved it in his pocket. "Yeah, course."

He didn't get to check it until he left later that afternoon, but Henry hadn't messaged him again.

Dom worried at his lip as he drove home.

Henry's texts had been a constant in his life since they'd left the holiday park. Dom was already used to their snarky and sometimes strange banter. He looked forward to it. Radio silence from Henry left Dom a little off-kilter.

When Nathan popped in later that night, Dom was so distracted he zoned out of their conversation completely.

"Are you all right?" Nathan asked, startling him into almost dropping his beer.

"What?" Dom blinked and realised Nathan had moved to lean against the worktop beside him.

Nathan gave a pointed look to the thick soup Dom was currently stirring. "You turned the heat off about five minutes ago. Are we actually going to eat at some point or are you going to stir it all night?"

"Fuck, sorry." He quickly dished up and they took their food to the table. He set his annoyingly quiet phone next to him.

"What's up? And don't say nothing, because I know that's bollocks."

"Fine." Dom rolled his eyes. "I might have messed things up with Henry. Maybe. I don't know."

Nathan paused with his spoon halfway to his mouth. "Holiday Henry?"

"Please don't call him that." It conjured up images of a grumpy Henry in his Christmas jumper and Dom laughed.

"Ooh," Nathan singsonged. "So it *is* him. I thought you weren't interested in seeing him again. Or have you changed your mind?"

Dom played with his soup. "I never said I wasn't interested," he said, watching his spoon intently.

"Dom." Nathan waited for him to look up. When he did, whatever expression Dom wore, made him sigh and set his spoon down. "What happened?"

Dom winced and handed his phone over for Nathan to read.

He skimmed through the last few messages. "How old did you say he was?"

"Twenty-six."

"Hmm."

His tone made Dom bristle. "What's that supposed to mean? Not everyone's fortunate enough to afford their own house these days."

Nathan cocked an eyebrow, and Dom snapped his mouth shut. "I know that. I was just thinking how knowing that *you* live alone *and* own your own house is probably a bit daunting when he's struggling to get his foot on the first rung of the ladder. So to speak."

"So you think I did mess up?"

Nathan reached for the bread and broke a bit off before answering. "Honestly? I have no idea."

"I'm so glad I confided in you. Your advice is priceless."

Nathan grinned. "You never listen to my advice anyway."

"I know, but usually it makes me realise that I'm better off following my original plan."

"Well, what's your plan this time?"

Dom set his spoon down with a sigh. "I don't know."

"You still like him though, right?"

"Yeah, I do." And after a week of seeing him every day, Dom missed him, but . . .

And there it was.

Did he want to pick up where they left off?

"I like this thing we've got going on." He gestured to his phone.

Nathan studied him for a long moment. "You like texting him when you could be fucking?"

Of course Dom missed the sex. Going from having Henry in his bed to his own hand wasn't the best, but what they were doing was . . . nice.

Dom shrugged, not wanting to explain how getting Henry's texts was the highlight of his day, and he was okay with just that for now.

Nathan's gaze softened. "You really do like him."

"Yeah."

"Okay. In that case, message him. Or maybe, I don't know, give him a call since texts can always be taken the wrong way."

"Yeah, maybe." Dom wasn't shy or nervous by any stretch of the imagination, but for whatever reason, the thought of speaking to Henry on the phone made his palms sweat.

By mutual agreement they moved on to safe topics for the rest of the evening. But Dom went to bed that night with every intention of calling Henry once he was settled. Unfortunately he fell asleep before he had chance and woke the next morning to his alarm and a missed opportunity.

Shit.

I really wanted to clear the air last night.

Reaching for his phone, Dom held his breath, only to let it out with a whoosh when he saw the waiting message. Sent at ten to six that morning.

Wow, Henry was up with the birds.

Henry: *Morning. Sorry about last night. I felt a bit awkward and not sure what to say.*

Dom typed and deleted his message about four times before hitting Send.

Dom: *That's ok. I hope I didn't sound like a condescending wanker?*

He didn't expect a reply immediately, so he set his phone down and got ready for work.

Henry replied at lunch time.

Henry: *No more than usual.*

It took Dom a minute to get his meaning, but before he had chance to be offended, his phone buzzed again.

Henry: *I'm joking! ;)*

The tension Dom had carried since he woke up melted away and he settled back into his seat, lunch forgotten.

Dom: *So, about your lack of Xmas decorations . . .*

Henry: *That's what I meant to ask you yesterday before I got all pissy and stomped off.*

Dom: *Is that what you did?*

Henry: *Kind of.*

Henry: *Anyway, we're going to get a tree on Saturday, but don't want to pay a fortune since we're poor ex-students. Or get a crap one that sheds its needles everywhere. And since you're an expert . . .*

Dom: *You want to know where to get one?*

Henry: *Yeah. I know you're way down in Somerset but figured you probably know places up here, right?*

Dom grinned at his phone.

Dom: *As it happens, I know just the place.*

———

THEY SPENT the rest of the week texting back and forth about all sorts of things that had Dom laughing throughout an otherwise gruelling workday. He'd broken his rule of keeping his phone on silent during the day, eager for Henry's messages.

Judging by the frequency that they now came, it seemed Henry had done the same.

If anyone noticed his sudden addiction to his phone, no one mentioned it.

Dom had Friday off, and Thursday evening couldn't come soon enough.

He was knackered.

Ducking under the sprigs of mistletoe adorning every door at work, Dom went in search of his brother to tell him he was done for the day.

His phone chimed, the familiar sound producing a smile

every time he heard it now. And sure enough, Henry's name lit up the screen.

Henry: *Hey, I know we haven't talked about this, but fuck it, I'm just going to ask anyway. Do you fancy meeting up? Coffee, beer anything. I'd really like to see you again.*

"Dom?" His mum called him from behind, and he turned to see her rushing down the path towards him, her harried expression having him instantly wary. "Oh, thank god I caught you."

"What's wrong?" Dom immediately slipped his phone back in his pocket and gave her his full attention.

"Your Uncle Mark's had an accident."

"Fuck, is he all right?"

She didn't even comment on his language, so he knew it wasn't going to be good news. "Broke his leg in two places. They've got to operate on it to fix things."

"Ouch." Mark was his dad's brother and they were alike in so many ways. Always active and would rather be outside than in. This was going to be torture for him.

He also owned a garden centre up in north Bristol very similar to theirs. Dom had a sinking feeling he knew what his mum was going to say next.

"You know how busy it gets this time of year, and with Mark out of action for a good few weeks . . ." She gave him a commiserating look. "I know it's not what you want to be doing especially this close to Christmas, and I wouldn't ask, but your brothers aren't as well rounded as you. Chrissy will need help with everything, and you're the first person I thought of."

He groaned.

Not that he minded helping out family, but he'd gone all out this year, decorating his house like a bloody scene from a Christmas card, and he'd hoped to have people round, not leave it empty as he spent the run up to Christmas in someone else's house.

His sigh must've spoken volumes because his mum put her hand on his arm.

"It's fine. I'll talk to your dad, we'll sort it out between us."

Yeah, that wasn't happening. His mum suffered on and off from a bad back and his dad had the start of arthritis in his hands. That was one of the reasons he and his brothers all worked there.

"It's fine, Mum."

"You sure? Because—"

"When do they need me?"

"Now." She laughed at his expression. "I know, I know. But Chrissy's in and out of the hospital visiting Mark, so she's not been in the shop much. They're struggling to keep everything running smoothly."

"How long for?" This was the part he was dreading most.

"Until the rush for trees dies off. Maybe the twenty-third, possibly twenty-fourth?"

Okay, he could live with that. his plan was to have a few friends over Christmas Eve, so as long as he could still do that, he was happy.

"Right. I'd better go pack, then."

So much for my day off tomorrow.

Henry sat slumped at the breakfast bar, phone in hand, staring at the message he'd sent Dom Thursday night.

Henry: *Hey, I know we haven't talked about this, but fuck it, I'm just going to ask anyway. Do you fancy meeting up? Coffee, beer anything. I'd really like to see you again.*

What had possessed him to send that?

You miss him.

He did. Their texts back and forth had only made him realise that he liked Dom. More than for sex. He made him laugh, which his mum had always told him was one of the most important things in a relationship.

And, yes, he was hot as fuck and Henry missed having his hands on him, but he missed cuddling up to him at night too.

Weird how you could get used to something over such a short time.

He sighed and reread the message for the hundredth time.

Way too fucking desperate.

He should've known after the first text when Dom didn't add an *x* to his reply. A small thing in theory but it had clearly spoken volumes.

Which Henry blissfully ignored.

Dom isn't interested in anything more.

His lack of a response to Henry's question made that glaringly obvious.

Fuck.

Why didn't I take the hint?

He knew this feeling, recognised it from when he'd caught Kyle cheating.

Stupid and embarrassed.

The texts that he'd thought of as them getting to know each other, connecting while apart, now took on a new meaning. Had Dom been humouring him? Replying to his ridiculous messages while thinking of a way to let him down gently?

He had to know how Henry felt. Subtlety wasn't his strong suit.

His phone buzzed with a message, and for one heart stopping moment, hope flared big and bright and Henry snatched his phone off the table.

Jason: Stuck at fucking work. Sorry. You still okay to get the tree? Mum's given us a box of decs so we're all set for later.

Great.

Henry sighed heavily and gave in to gravity, resting his head on the breakfast bar. The very last thing he felt like doing was picking out a Christmas tree. His festive spirit had grown wings and flown away.

In his current mood, he'd end up with some shitty, spindly thing with no needles. But if he didn't get one today the likelihood was they wouldn't get one at all since they'd left it to the last minute anyway.

Fuck going on his own though.

Knowing an inquisition was coming his way but not having the energy to care, Henry messaged his sister.

AN HOUR later they were on the road. The sky was that ominous heavy white-grey colour that promised snow.

Henry wasn't in the mood for that either.

Finally they pulled into the garden centre Dom had suggested. Henry had baulked at the idea at first, but Google said it was one of the best near him, so he'd put his pettiness aside and here they were.

It was busy.

Way busier than he'd expected this close to Christmas.

"It's the eighteenth of December. Shouldn't everyone have got their trees by now?" He huffed, waiting for someone to leave so he could nab their parking space.

Ella shifted in her seat to stare at him, eyebrows raised.

"What? I'm young, I'm allowed to be behind in these things." He waved at the couples and families wandering about perusing trees. "What's their excuse?"

Ella ignored his grumbling. "Why are you in such a pissy mood?"

"I'm not." He saw her eyes narrow in his periphery and kept his glued to the car reversing in front of them.

"Heard from Dom lately?"

He winced before he could catch himself and Ella sat back in her seat with an "Ahh."

"What does that mean?"

"It means I know there's something wrong with your 'no-strings'"—she actually used air quotes—"bf, so just tell me and I can commiserate and then call you an arse."

"What makes you think it's my fault?"

"Because you've got a squirrelly look about you."

"I have not." He even felt squirrelly.

"You so do. So either it was your fault, or it wasn't but you're blaming yourself anyway."

"Fuck's sake, I really hate how you know me so well."

She laughed, squeezing his arm. "No you don't. Hurry up and park, then you can tell Ella all about it."

Henry grimaced. "Never talk about yourself in the third person again." He shuddered. "You sound creepy."

He pulled into the free space and turned the engine off. His very silent phone sat tucked in his pocket. He could just show her the message thread, but he couldn't bring himself to look at it again, let alone show it to someone else. Even his sister.

"Come on, I'll tell you while we pick a bloody tree." After locking the car, he fell into step beside her. "It's pretty boring, though. Don't get all excited."

"Nothing is ever boring with you, Hen."

Apparently Dom thinks so.

Probably.

"Don't call me that," he groused. "I'm not five."

"You act it."

"When?" He stopped abruptly and glared at her, making her laugh. Crossing his arms made her laugh even more, and a reluctant smile tugged at his lips. "Oh fuck off." He marched in the direction of some Nordic Firs, ignoring her calls for him to wait.

"I'm sorry," she said, catching up to him and looping her arm through his. "What happened? I thought you were happily getting to know him through texts?"

Henry frowned. "It sounds shit when you put it like that."

She pinched his side, making him startle. "No, I think it's a good idea. You had a no-strings arrangement. So while you probably had a lot of sex, you can't really get to know each other well in a week. No matter how much time you spent together."

"I suppose."

"Makes sense to take a little time communicating before taking things further."

Who is this person and what have they done with my sister?

As if reading his mind, Ella glanced over at him. "What? I know things!"

By mutual agreement, they stopped in front of a pile of trees and started the arduous task of sorting through everyone else's leftovers.

Henry dutifully held up tree after tree while Ella squinted at them, then invariably shook her head. "I don't think Dom was interested in seeing me again."

Ella stopped inspecting the tree he held and looked at him. "What makes you say that? I thought you said you got the feeling he really liked you."

"I did." He ran a hand through his hair, glancing up at the sky when it felt damp. "Is it snowing?"

"Barely." Ella motioned with her hands for Henry to continue.

Henry bit his lip, not wanting to sound ridiculous, but he let the words spill out anyway. "I put a kiss on my first message and he didn't send one back."

Oh kill me now. That sounded so much better in my head.

Ella stared at him, lips twitching.

"Yes, fine, laugh it up." He glared at her as she failed to stifle giggles.

"I'm sorry, but is that it? Really?"

"Of course that's not it. And yeah, it might sound stupid to focus on that one thing, but I think it says a great deal. I have to actively stop myself adding kisses to Jason's texts, let alone someone I'm fucking."

A shocked "Honestly!" from behind had him closing his eyes and counting to ten while Ella apologised on his behalf.

Why me?

When the offended lady had moved away, Henry carried on. "My point is, adding a kiss is force of habit for most people."

"So you think he didn't add an x on purpose?" She still didn't look convinced by Henry's reasoning.

"Yes. So as not to encourage me." He set the tree down and scrubbed a hand over his face, groaning when his gloves were a little sticky with tree sap.

Awesome.

"I just got the feeling that he'd rather leave it as a holiday fling and not take it any further."

Ella took a moment to ruminate over his words. "Not to disparage your gut instinct or anything, but is that the only reason you think he doesn't want to see you again?"

Henry toed the ground, gaze fixed on his boots. "Well, that and the fact that I asked him if he wanted to meet up and he didn't answer."

"Oh."

That one word made his heart sink like a stone. "Yeah."

"When did you ask him?"

"Thursday. I sent him a message on my break."

Since it was now Saturday, the odds weren't good that Henry was getting an answer that he wanted.

She offered him a sympathetic smile. "Maybe he's been busy?"

Henry shrugged. "It's possible. But he's always replied to my other messages, even if it was later in the evening." Shoving his hands in his pockets, Henry rocked back on his heels before voicing something he really didn't want to. "I think it's more likely that he's not interested in seeing me again and either can't think of a nice way to tell me, or this *is* him telling me."

The snow had got heavier, much like Henry's heart, and he tilted his face to the sky, letting the flakes land on his cold cheeks. "It was just sex between two people who didn't really know each other at all. No strings, no feelings, no repeat."

A sharp intake of breath alerted him they weren't alone, and Henry threw his hands in the air. "For fuck's sake," he muttered. "Can't I catch a fucking break?" He whirled round to apologise to yet another offended individual, but the words died on his tongue.

"Dom?"

"Henry."

Henry stood there, unable to articulate anything other than that. His initial delight at seeing Dom soon morphed into hurt, then anger. "What are you doing here?" It came out way more accusatory than he'd intended, but Dom said he lived in Somerset. Had he lied?

"Working." Far from looking guilty about ignoring Henry's message, Dom seemed hurt, and if Henry wasn't mistaken, a little pissed off.

What the hell does he have to be pissed off about? Henry thought indignantly.

And then Dom's words sank in. *Work? Here? What the hell was going on?*

Narrowing his eyes, Henry said, "How come you're working here if you live in Somerset?"

A little voice suggested that maybe Dom had told him to get his tree here so that Henry would come see him. Maybe he'd planned to surprise him?

The sour expression on Dom's face made that seem highly unlikely, so Henry quashed that line of thinking immediately. Dom hadn't known what day Henry was planning on visiting, and he couldn't be at work all the time.

Anger raised its ugly head again, and before Dom had a chance to answer, Henry blurted out the one question he really wanted an answer to. "Why did you ignore my text? If you didn't want to see me again, you could've just said so, instead of leaving me waiting for two days wondering if I'd ever hear from you again."

Dom's eyes widened for a moment, then he stared at Henry for a good few moments before speaking. "Why did you want to see me again if it was just sex between two people who didn't really know each other at all? No strings, no feelings, no repeat." He raised an eyebrow and Henry squirmed in place.

Fuck.

"You heard that."

"I did."

Henry sucked his bottom lip between his teeth, anger draining away as fast as it had appeared. Embarrassment and a little confusion replaced it. Was that why Dom was angry? Because he thought Henry didn't give a shit?

Dom shoved his hands in his pockets but didn't take his eyes off Henry. "Is that why you asked to see me again? For sex?"

Henry quickly glanced around them, but naturally no one was there when it wasn't him speaking. "No, of course not. And I know how that sounded, but if you only heard that last bit, then you've got it totally out of context."

Dom crossed his arms and Henry's gaze flicked to the tattoos peeking out from his coat sleeves. "Explain it to me then."

"I was telling Ella that's how I thought you felt." Until that moment, Henry had forgotten all about his sister. Both his and Dom's gaze swung round to land on Ella where she stood watching them, eyes like saucers.

"Oh, don't mind me." She waved at them to continue, and Henry scowled at her before facing Dom again.

He took off his gloves, not risking sap hair again, and rubbed the back of his neck, wondering what to say to fix this. "When you didn't reply to my text, I thought you didn't want to see me, and either you couldn't find a good way to tell me, or just couldn't be arsed."

"Seriously?"

Henry suddenly had the feeling he'd monumentally cocked this up, just not in the way he'd first thought. "I—"

"If that's what you thought of me, then maybe you were right. We really don't know each other at all." He gave Henry a long, considering look. "Goodbye, Henry." With a small shake of his head, Dom turned and walked away.

Henry stood rooted to the spot, mouth hanging open. "*Shit.*"

"Don't just stand there like an idiot," Ella hissed, giving him a not-so-gentle nudge. "Go after him."

"I don't think—"

"No, you don't, and that's your problem."

Henry glared at her, but maybe she had a point.

"*Go,*" she hissed again, reminding Henry of a spitting Cobra, coiled and ready to strike. Probably wise to get away, even if he wasn't sure Dom would be any more welcoming.

And how fast did he fucking walk?

Henry ran to catch up with him, a little out of breath by the time he was close enough to slide in front of him. "I'm sorry."

Dom came to an abrupt halt but still almost bowled Henry over. He grabbed Henry's shoulders to stop him toppling over backwards. His scowl was still there, but Henry thought he saw the faintest twitch of his lips.

When Dom didn't say anything, Henry realised with a sinking feeling this was all going to be on him.

Well, you were the one with all the assumptions.

He checked around to make sure whatever came out of his mouth wouldn't offend anyone and noticed, for the first time, that they were in a little secluded spot behind a building he suspected might be the café. Out of sight of most people.

He took a deep breath.

Here goes.

"I'm sorry I jumped to conclusions. It was never just sex for me. Those seven days together were some of the best I've ever had, but while we do know each other in some ways, I guess we are strangers in others."

Dom listened but said nothing.

Okay then.

"I missed seeing you every day, and I know it's only been two weeks, but I didn't want to lose the connection we'd made because I really like you. I wasn't sure how you felt, though. You didn't return the kiss on my first text." *Oh no, Henry, stop talking right now.*

That got an eyebrow raise.

"Not knowing where we stood was killing me, so I took the plunge and asked you if you wanted to meet up. When you didn't reply . . . well, I took it to mean you weren't interested." He held his arms out wide. "And here we are."

"Yes, here we are." Dom said, although Henry was none the wiser as to what was going on in his head. His expression softened and Henry held his breath. "I'm not sure which point to address first." He sighed, breath misty in the chilly morning air.

"I'm going to be honest with you, Henry . . ."

Oh. Henry's heart stuttered. Any hope he had died a quick death because surely, that didn't bode well.

"When we left the holiday park, I wasn't sure I wanted to see you again."

Fuck.

He might have thought something along those lines, but hearing Dom say it out loud *hurt.* "I see. Right . . . um . . . I guess I'll just . . ." He started to back away, face flushed with embarrassment and his heart somewhere near his boots.

"Wait." Dom's hand shot out to grab his arm before he could get far. "I wasn't finished."

Oh great, there's more.

Henry mentally steeled himself for whatever else Dom had to say.

"It wasn't you." Dom paused, and Henry rolled his eyes. *Oh, how original.* "Well, no, I guess it was. But—"

He couldn't help it, he laughed. All pitchy and slightly manic. Because, really? "I'm going to find my sister." He tried for the second time to march off with the shreds of his dignity, but again Dom stopped him.

"I'm sorry I'm not explaining this well, but it's been a long two days and I'm really fucking tired." He ran a hand over his face, and Henry took a good long look at him. Only then did he notice the shadows under his eyes and the tight set to his shoulders.

"Is this a café?" Henry gestured at the building behind them. "Would you . . . um . . . like to get a coffee with me?" The wind chose that moment to make itself known and Henry shivered.

Dom smiled for the first time since Henry had run into him, and it felt like the sun coming out. "Yeah, okay. I think we could both do with one."

Henry didn't have a clue where this conversation was headed, but talking had to be good, right?

He let Dom lead the way and followed him inside.

CHAPTER 10

Dom smiled in greeting at Lucy standing behind the counter.

Turning to Henry, he asked, "What would you like to drink?"

"Er . . . just a regular coffee's fine, thanks."

Walking to the edge of the counter, Dom said, "Two flat whites when you've got a minute, Luce." She gave him a thumbs up and went back to serving the couple at the till.

The café was packed, so Dom steered Henry to the back where there was a small table reserved for staff. It was a little out of the way and afforded them a modicum of privacy.

This wasn't where he thought they'd have this conversation, but if they didn't clear things up between them now, Dom didn't think they ever would.

No sooner had they sat down than their coffees appeared.

"Christ, that was fast." Henry took his coffee, thanking Lucy for bringing it over.

"It's who you know." Dom wrapped his fingers around his mug and inhaled the steam. "I needed this." The warmth of the café seeped into him, and he yawned, jaw cracking.

"Why are you so tired? And why are you here?" Henry fiddled

with the handle of his mug before looking up to meet Dom's gaze. "I don't understand."

Dom sighed and took a quick sip of his drink. He needed a shot of caffeine before tackling this. "My aunt and uncle own this place." He gestured around them.

Henry's eyes widened. "Green fingers run in the family, then."

"Something like that." He took another sip of coffee before setting his mug on the table. "My uncle Mark broke his leg on Wednesday. He had an operation yesterday to fix it, so he'll be out of action for the foreseeable future. My aunt's been back and forth from the hospital, so she's hardly been here either. My mum asked me to come help out in the run up to Christmas."

"Oh." Henry seemed to shrink into his seat. "I'm sorry about your uncle."

"Thanks. He's going to be fine. Eventually." Dom waited until Henry was looking at him again before continuing. "I left Thursday evening to come straight here, and I've been run off my feet ever since. That's why I haven't replied to your message yet."

Henry bit his lip, eyes back on his mug. "*Fuck*. I'm sorry for getting so dramatic over everything. I feel like such a dick."

"Hey." Dom reached across the table and grasped Henry's hand. "I'm sorry too. I shouldn't have left you wondering where we stood with each other."

"What you said," Henry began, fingers tight around Dom's. "About it being my fault. What did you mean?"

Dom winced and inwardly cursed his tired fucking brain. That whole sentence had come out wrong. He sipped his coffee, giving himself time to work out exactly what he wanted to say.

He'd had a vague idea of what he was going to say to Henry when they finally met up, but hearing him describe them as nothing more than *strangers who'd fucked* had thrown him a bit.

"Look, I don't have the best track record with partners. My last two relationships ended because we weren't at the same place in our lives. They weren't ready to settle down . . ." He shrugged, wondering if he was about to scare Henry off. "And I was. Still am."

He watched Henry, trying to gauge his reaction, but for once his expression gave nothing away. He tapped the side of his mug, the only indication he was anything other than calm.

"So I was right. My crap job and the fact I still share a house put you off asking to see me again." The edge to his tone made Dom feel guilty, and he rushed to explain himself better.

"No, I don't give a shit about those things."

Do I?

No, he really didn't.

"It was more the fact that you're younger than me—"

Henry scoffed, and Dom sighed.

"I know six years isn't loads, but you've only recently finished uni. You're just starting out, and I didn't want to risk getting involved with someone only to find out yet again that we weren't at the same place in life."

Henry's eyes narrowed, and now it was easy for Dom to tell he was pissed off. "So without bothering to talk to me at all, you decided all on your own that the fact I went to uni later than most people meant pursuing anything with me was a waste of time and effort."

Dom opened his mouth, but Henry was far from done.

"If you didn't want to see me again because it was only a holiday fling for you, I would've accepted that and moved on. I'd have been a little gutted because I thought we had something, but it is what it is." He snatched his hand out of Dom's. "This, though?" He gestured between them. "Is so much worse. I've been judged and found wanting, all because I took the time to live a little and earn some money so I wouldn't be riddled with debt when I left uni."

Dom stared at him. It had been a long time since someone had put him in his place so thoroughly. And, he had to admit, rightly so. Dom prided himself on not being a judgy fucker, on not making assumptions, and always looking at both sides of things. When had that changed?

"You're absolutely right." He sat back in his chair with a heavy sigh, annoyed with himself and wondering how the hell to sort this mess out.

Because one thing he did know was that he couldn't let Henry walk out of there without trying to fix this mess between them.

"I'm sorry for doing that." Taking a chance, he reached for Henry's hand again, beyond relieved when Henry let him take it.

"But you were right with what you said outside earlier. We don't really know each other."

"You know I didn't mean—"

Dom stopped him with a raised hand. "Yeah, I do, and the rest of it was bollocks." He shot Henry a small smile to take the sting out of his words. "We know a *version* of each other, a carefree holiday version that isn't the same as how we are in everyday life."

Henry sighed. "Yeah, I guess that's true." He had a defeated look about him, and Dom barrelled on desperate to change that.

He squeezed Henry's fingers. "That doesn't mean I don't want to get to know you better."

"Really?"

Scepticism laced his voice, but the spark of hope in his eyes made Dom's stomach flutter. Nerves and excitement warred inside him as he wondered for the hundredth time if he was doing the right thing.

I am.

Even if it scares me.

"Yeah," he said, smile growing wider by the second. "Really."

Henry's small smile took a while to appear, but eventually it won out. "I'd like that too."

They stared at each other, holding hands and smiling, until Dom remembered they weren't actually alone but sat in a crowded café. He had to work with some of these people, and while he knew none of them would give him shit for being with a bloke, they wouldn't hesitate to take the piss out of him for holding hands and getting sappy in the middle of a garden centre coffee shop.

That said, Dom couldn't bring himself to let go of Henry's fingers. Or stop smiling.

"Sooo . . ." Henry looked at him, blue eyes bright with happiness but also a trace of uncertainty. Like he thought this was all going to change any second. "What happens now?"

Now Dom would like nothing better than to take Henry home with him and get properly reacquainted. Except he wasn't staying at home at the minute, and his gut told him they should maybe take their time before rushing back in. Actually get to know each other instead of just talking about it.

"I'm staying with my aunt until Christmas Eve."

Henry frowned, and yeah, that wasn't exactly an answer to his question.

"So we could meet for a drink after work or something if you wanted. I'm probably going to be too knackered for much else." He hoped Henry got his meaning without having to spell it out.

"A drink sounds good," Henry answered, a look of understanding in his eyes. "When?" He bit his lip. "Sorry, I don't mean to put you on the spot, but we've already established I have no patience."

And after everything Dom had told him, he probably didn't trust Dom to follow through with it.

And I don't blame him.

Dom ran through his work schedule in his head. This close to Christmas, every day was exhausting, but no way was he leaving this till afterwards. "How about Monday night?"

"I finish at six, but I can meet you about seven, seven-thirty if you want?"

"Yeah, perfect." Dom checked his watch, surprised at how long they'd been sat there. "Shit, I'm really sorry, but I need to get back to work."

Henry's eyes widened. "And I left my sister outside in the cold. *Fuck.*" He pushed his chair back and stood. "She's going to kill me."

They hurried to the door, the cold air hitting them like a slap in the face when they stepped outside.

Dom hesitated, unsure. It felt far too much like the last time they parted ways and he didn't want a repeat of that.

Tugging Henry to one side, he remembered something he'd said earlier. "Before you go." Dom grabbed his hand and drew him close. "I'm sorry I didn't add a kiss to that very first message."

Henry blushed a lovely shade of pink. "Oh god, please forget I ever mentioned that."

Dom smirked. "It's burnt into my brain."

"Along with every other time I've made an arse of myself, I'm sure."

"The truth is, I was deciding whether or not to add one, then I hit Send by mistake."

Henry huffed out a laugh. "I'm not sure that's any better."

"If I could go back and change it, I would."

He cupped Henry's jaw and leant in, waiting that split second for him to pull way if he didn't want this. His small smile was all Dom got before Henry closed the last bit of distance between them and kissed him.

His arms snapped around Dom's waist. The many layers of clothing between them prevented them from getting too close, but this was enough and Dom melted into it. Cold lips met his, but Henry's mouth was warm and inviting. The rough stubble on his cheeks an added thrill that set his pulse racing. The sweep of Henry's tongue, the soft moan that escaped him, all of it unlocking a door inside Dom that had held him back from letting himself have this.

Have Henry.

But now that door was wide open and whatever happened, Dom knew he'd made the right decision.

Henry walked back to his car with a huge smile on his face. Yes, he'd behaved like a bit of a twat these past two days, but everything was fine now.

Way more than fine, actually.

"Oh, I'm glad to see someone's happy." Ella stood next to Henry's car, a wrapped Christmas tree propped up next to her as she glared at him with her arms crossed.

Arse.

I've got the car keys.

"Shit, I'm sorry, El." He rushed to unlock the car and sorted out securing the tree to the roof of his car while Ella scrambled inside and slammed the door hard enough to make Henry wince.

After double-checking the tree wasn't going anywhere, he took a deep breath and joined her inside.

"That was Dom."

"No shit." She rolled her eyes for good measure. "I'm glad to see your taste in men has improved, though." The smirk she sent his way told him she wasn't all that mad, and Henry relaxed against the seat, his smile returning.

"*Oohh.*"

"Oh, what?"

She got a knowing look on her face and Henry shifted uncomfortably. "You like him. As in *really* like him."

"I already told you that," Henry mumbled, starting the car for some much-needed heat.

"You told me you spent the week together having lots of sex. I figured you wanted to meet up again to carry that on. Not that you like him, *like* him.

"You make me sound like a fifteen-year-old with a crush."

"Sorry, I'm just in shock."

"Why?" He noticed someone waiting for his space, so he carefully backed out and pulled onto the road.

"Well, and don't get pissy at me for saying this, but it's not all that long since you broke up with Kyle and you swore you weren't dating ever again."

"That was ages ago." *Wasn't it?*

It sure as fuck felt like ages since Kyle had been a part of his life.

"About six weeks." Ella worked it out for him. "And I'm not saying that Dom is just rebound sex, but . . ."

"That's exactly what you're saying, right?" He glanced at her and she had the grace to look guilty.

"Fine," Henry conceded. "The thought had crossed my mind. And maybe at first that's exactly what it was."

"But?" Ella prompted.

But now it was so much more than that. When Henry thought about Kyle, he barely got irritated. Kyle had done him a favour, because Henry doubted whether he'd have got around to ending things any time soon if he hadn't been forced to.

Looking at it now, it was easy to see they hadn't been right for each other. Or all that good together.

"Dom's nothing like Kyle."

"And thank fuck for that."

Henry laughed as she shuddered in her seat. "He's older, for one."

"Kyle never did act his age."

"That's true. But I'm not saying Dom acts like an old man or anything. He's only six years older than me, but he's sooo . . . together. Do you know what I mean?"

"Because he has a good job and a house?" She raised an eyebrow. "You sound like you're shopping for a prospective husband, not describing your smoking hot bf."

Henry reached over and gave her a shove. "That's not what I

meant. It's just . . ." He glanced over at her, wondering how much he wanted to share. Telling Ella would make it all that much more real somehow. "He knows I live with three other guys, that I work at Tesco, and only just finished my degree, and he doesn't care."

"And why the fuck should he?"

Ahh, Ella. Always in my corner. Got to love her.

"Thank you, and you're right, but I meant it's more of a non-issue. It was me who was all hung up about it."

"Shocker," she said, laughing.

Henry scowled at her.

I take it all back.

He sighed as he finally pulled into his driveway. "I really like him, El. It's just all so new and tentative, I'm worried I'll say the wrong thing and fuck it up." Despite Dom's words to the contrary, Henry couldn't help but wonder if deep down Dom still thought of him as a bad bet.

Henry went to get out of the car, but Ella stopped him with her hand on his arm. "Look. I don't know what the two of you talked about, but you went from ashen-faced when you ran after him to positively beaming when you got back, so it must've been good." She smiled at him. "Just be you, Henry. That's all you have to do." She shrugged and reached for the door handle. "If it doesn't work out, then he isn't the one for you."

His eyes narrowed. "You read that somewhere, didn't you?"

She slapped his arm but laughed, so he knew he was right. "I might've done, but it's still true. Now let's get this tree inside and you can thank me for picking such a beauty while you were off getting cosy with your boy toy."

Henry snorted. "If anyone's the—" He stopped abruptly, not wanting to put that idea in his sister's head, but judging by the twinkle in her eye, the damage was done.

"Oh, you so are, aren't you?" She laughed all the way to his front door and Henry shook his head as he undid the straps on the tree. He heard voices behind him and prayed Ella hadn't said anything to his housemates. But then he remembered her face when he got back to the car earlier. Her lips had almost been blue.

Yeah, no way she was keeping quiet.

"Want a hand?" Jason walked towards him, whistling at the size of the tree. "Looks like you might need it."

"Yeah, thanks."

Jason walked round to the back of the car to get the end of the tree. "I hear you've sorted things out with your sugar daddy."

Henry looked up to see Jason grinning widely.

"Oh, fuck off."

Payback was indeed a bitch.

DECORATING the tree turned out to be less of a ball ache than Henry anticipated. True to his word, Jason had more Christmas decorations than they would ever need, courtesy of his mum, and with the aid of beer, the four of them and Ella made a valiant effort at trimming the tree.

"There." Ella stepped back, hands on her hips. "I think that'll do."

Thank god, because Henry was done.

Looking around at his housemates, they were of the same opinion. But when Ella hurried over to turn off the living room lights, even Henry had to admit it looked amazing.

Multi-coloured fairy lights wound around the tree, making the red and green baubles glitter and shine. A star sat on top, a little wonky now Henry looked closely at it, but he kind of liked it that way.

The overall effect was stunning. It brought a whole new warmth to their living area and some Christmas cheer that had been sadly lacking. Henry pulled out his phone and snapped a picture. It took him several attempts to get a halfway decent one, and it still didn't do the tree justice, but it would have to do.

Henry: *Festive spirit is present at last!*

He attached the photo and hit Send.

Knowing Dom was probably busy, Henry set his phone aside and spent the evening getting steadily tipsy with his housemates and his sister, all the while quietly admiring their new tree and replaying his chat with Dom.

HENRY WAS in bed by the time Dom's reply came through.

Dom: *That looks great. Must've been a great place you got it from ;)*

Henry: *It wasn't bad. Staff weren't all that helpful though. One guy kept me talking so long, my sister ended up picking it on her own.*

Dom: *Shit. I totally should've helped you pick out a tree. Sorry!*

Henry: *I was kidding! Seriously, Ella would've picked it out anyway. She has a far better eye than me.*

Dom: *I think you've got beautiful eyes.*

Dom: *Shit, that sounded cheesy. In my defence, I'm knackered, I'm not at my best.*

Henry: *So you're saying I've not got beautiful eyes? I'm hurt.*

Henry grinned to himself as he stared at the screen waiting for Dom's reply. He didn't have to wait long.

Dom: *I love your eyes, Henry. They remind me of warm summer days with cloudless skies. I get lost in them sometimes when I look at you.*

Henry swallowed past the sudden lump in his throat. That might be the nicest thing anyone had ever said to him. He stared at the words, heart thundering against his ribcage, and despite telling himself Dom was probably just messing with him, Henry clung to the warm feeling they evoked inside him.

Dom: *Too much?*

In his rush to reply, Henry fumbled his phone, sending a stream of nonsense.

Fuck.

Dom: *I didn't know you had a cat?*

Henry: *I wish I could blame it on someone else. I almost dropped my phone. And no, not too much,* he typed quickly, not wanting Dom to think it had been too much and try and gloss over it.

Henry: *Perfect actually.*

Ugh, he cringed rereading his own message. That probably *was* too much though.

Dom: *Good. I meant every word.*

Dom: *And as much as I want to stay up talking to you, I need to be up at six tomorrow. I'm really looking forward to Monday.*

Although a little disappointed about not getting chance to talk more, Henry's smile remained huge as he clutched his phone tight. This was so much more than he'd expected when he'd got up that morning.

Henry: *Me too. Night, Dom x*

He hit Send, holding his breath for Dom's reply. It popped up two seconds later and Henry's heart swelled as he read it.

Dom: *Night, Henry x*

That little x at the end might be a small thing, but to Henry it was *everything*.

AFTER SPENDING two days with no contact from Dom, Henry's phone was in his hand all day Sunday, and Monday he snuck into the toilet so many times to check for messages, his co-workers thought he had a dodgy belly.

Monday night Henry met Dom at a country pub about halfway between Henry's house and Dom's aunt's. They could've met at one of the gay bars in the city centre, but Henry figured

Dom would be knackered from work so had suggested somewhere closer.

He'd never had a problem at this pub, and it wasn't as though they were going to fuck over the table or anything.

Although as soon as that thought passed through his head, that was all he could think about doing, and keeping his hands to himself was torture. Despite that, it was a good evening.

Meeting somewhere like that forced them to talk.

Really talk.

And Henry found himself falling a little bit more under Dom's spell.

They parted with a quick kiss goodnight in the car park, and although Henry's cock would've been more than happy to follow Dom home, it was nice for once to have an evening that didn't revolve around sex.

Oh, who was he kidding?

He would totally have had sex if Dom had offered.

But he hadn't, even Henry could see how tired he was, but it still meant Henry crawled into his bed that night with an erection that wouldn't go away on its own.

He reached for his phone without a second thought.

Henry: *It was great to see you, but I now have a hard on and it's all your fault.*

Dom:*? I never touched you.*

Henry: *Exactly!*

Dom: *I think those old ladies next to us might've objected to me giving you a blow job under the table.*

Henry closed his eyes on a groan, one hand automatically reaching for his cock. His breath hitched after the first stroke, and it took all his effort to stop and reply to Dom's text.

Henry: *Thanks. You've just made it 10 times worse. And those ladies swore like sailors. I doubt they'd have batted an eye.*

The three dots appeared then disappeared, and Henry gave

himself another few firm strokes while he waited, heat blossoming in his belly.

Dom: *Are you touching yourself?*

Henry's heart stuttered, then set off at a gallop. He read the message twice to make sure he hadn't imagined it.

How the fuck did he know?

Henry bit his lip, wondering whether to admit to it.

Fuck it.

Henry: *Yeah. I'm so fucking hard thinking about you. I miss sleeping next to you.*

He debated deleting the last bit, thumb hovering over the button, afraid he'd scare Dom off. But Ella had said to be himself, and Henry wasn't lying. He did miss him.

He hit Send, then held his breath as he waited for Dom's response. It came way quicker than he expected.

Dom: *Fuck, Henry. I wish I was there with you.*

Henry: *What would you do?*

Excitement flowed through his veins, anticipation grabbing a hold of him, making his pulse race.

Dom: *You know what I like, Henry.*

I do.

Dom: *We'd be naked. You lying on your back, ready for me. I'd kiss my way down that glorious body of yours, tease your happy trail with my tongue.*

Henry swallowed, mouth dry.

Henry: *And then what?*

Dom: *Then I'd take your cock in my mouth, swallow you down until you hit the back of my throat.*

Oh god.

Henry had his fingers wrapped around his length, hips thrusting off the bed, pushing through his fist with a strangled cry.

Henry: *Close*

It was all he could manage one-handed, concentration shot as he jacked himself off.

Dom: *Me too. Wish I could watch you come. Fuck you with my fingers while I suck your cock.*

And I'm done.

Henry dropped his phone, clamped one hand over his mouth to stifle his cry, and stroked himself once, twice, and then he was coming, pleasure sweeping through him, lighting him up inside like it was Dom wringing every last shudder and moan out of him instead of his own hand.

Fuck.

He'd never come that hard on his own.

His phone buzzed with a text, and he snatched it up.

Dom: *Did you come?*

Henry: *Yeah. So fucking hard.*

Dom: *Good.*

Henry: *You?*

Dom: *Not yet.*

Henry: *Need some help?*

Not waiting for Dom's answer, Henry took a photo of his come-covered stomach and added the caption, *I was thinking of you.*

His phone remained silent for another minute or so, and Henry lay back on his pillow to enjoy the afterglow of an amazing orgasm. His cock gave an interested twitch as he pictured Dom getting off to his photo, but there was no way Henry was getting hard any time soon. That had wiped him out.

When Dom's text finally came through, Henry was already smiling as he opened it.

Dom: *Thanks for that. I almost jizzed on my phone.*

Henry laughed, feeling lighter than he had in days.

An orgasm will do that for you.

Henry: *Sorry.*

He totally wasn't.

Dom: *It was one of the hottest things I've seen. I bet you're not the least bit sorry.*

Henry: *No.*

Dom: *Me neither.*

Dom: *All I want now is to curl up with my arms around you and fall asleep.*

Oh god. I want that too.

Henry: *Sounds good.*

Maybe they could do that soon. Henry hoped that's where they were headed. Since their chat in the café on Saturday, it felt like they were on the same page now.

As if reading his mind, Dom's next text made his belly flutter and his heart clench.

Dom: *I know we should probably take things slow after the way we started. But I don't think I can. I miss falling asleep with you and waking up with you in my arms. I hope we can do that again.*

Henry: *Me too.*

Dom: *Soon.*

Henry: *I'd like that.*

He yawned, tiredness hitting him suddenly. Dom wasn't the only one knackered from work.

As much as he wanted to keep talking to Dom all night, Henry knew he was fighting a losing battle.

Henry: *I need to sleep.*

Dom: *Same. Night, Henry. x*

Henry: *Night, Dom x*

CHAPTER 11

Dom didn't begrudge helping his aunt and uncle, far from it, but to say he was looking forward to going home was an understatement.

Sexting with Henry had been awesome, but having a wank in the bedroom next to his Aunt Chrissy's wasn't something he wanted to repeat.

Ever.

He'd had trouble looking her in the eye the next morning.

But going home meant he'd be that much further away from Henry.

It sucked that they were so near each other now but couldn't make the most of it.

Dom supposed he could have gone round to Henry's house, but he didn't trust himself not to march Henry right up to his bedroom, and he'd rather not fuck Henry in a house he shared with three others.

At least not at first.

He wanted to take his time when they eventually took that step.

Again.

And Henry wasn't exactly quiet during sex.

"What's that face for? I thought you were loved up, now?" Nathan stood in front of him, hat on, coat zipped up to his neck but smiling wide.

Dom grinned and pulled him in for a hug. "What the fuck are you doing here?" He belatedly glanced around to make sure none of the public had wandered back this far, but they were safe.

"I was up this way and thought I'd come take you for lunch. Chrissy said she can spare you for an hour."

"She's here?" Dom frowned. "I thought she was taking Mark to the hospital this morning."

"She said they've just got back. Your uncle Mark's at the house and she'll take over here so you can have a break." He ushered Dom along. "Come on, I'm starving."

They ended up at a pub just down the road.

The Christmas tree in the entry way was a beauty and the pub itself was tastefully decorated, but Dom could've done without the Christmas soundtrack. After listening to the same songs for the last few weeks, he was about ready to scream.

He ordered their food while Nathan got the drinks.

"So," Nathan said as soon as they were both seated. "How's it going with Henry?"

Dom had filled him in on the weekend's events but he'd kept Monday night to himself. That didn't stop a rush of heat from creeping into his cheeks. "Good."

Nathan raised an eyebrow. "I'd say better than *good*, judging by that blush you've got going on. You two back at it?"

Dom sighed. "Not exactly. I can't bring him back to Chrissy's place, and he's got three housemates."

"Ahh." Realisation dawned far too quickly for Dom's liking. Nathan gave a pointed look at Dom's phone. "Good old sexting."

Dom snorted and rolled his eyes.

"I'm just saying it'll do the job in a pinch."

Well, Dom could hardly deny that.

"When are you seeing him again?"

He played with one of the beer mats on their table. "I don't know. I don't leave here until Christmas Eve." He sighed, already resigned to the fact he wouldn't be seeing Henry any time soon. "So after Christmas, I guess, or maybe even New Year's."

Nathan took a drink of his beer, then put it down with way too much care. That was his thinking face.

Dom braced himself.

"What are you doing for Christmas?"

"Same as usual. Going to my mum and dad's for lunch with everyone else. Why?"

"What are you doing Christmas Eve?"

Dom's eyes narrowed, but he answered. "You and Luke were supposed to be coming round."

Nathan waved him off. "You only asked us because you didn't want to be on your own after Sam."

That was sort of true. A few months ago he'd had plans of spending a romantic night in on Christmas Eve with Sam. Strangely, the thought didn't sting like he expected.

Huh.

He sat back in his chair. "Are you telling me you've got a better offer?"

Nathan smirked. "No, I'm saying that you have. Invite Henry instead."

Dom scoffed. "I can't do that."

"Why not? You want to see him again, and I can tell the thought of waiting until after New Year's depresses you. So why not ask him?"

"Pretty sure he'll have plans for Christmas Eve. It's only two days away."

"You won't know unless you ask him." Nathan set his glass down and fixed Dom with the look that he hated. The one that said he knew Dom was making up excuses and that he should just do it already. "What's the worst that can happen? He says he's busy." Nathan shrugged and sat back in his seat.

Dom shook his head and sent Nathan a mock glare. "I hate it when you do that."

"What? State the obvious?"

"Whatever. I'm not going to ask him."

His fingers itched to send Henry a message right that second.

"Mm-hmm."

To Dom's surprise, Nathan let the subject drop and the conversation moved on.

But it stayed in Dom's mind all through his afternoon at work. By the time he finished, his phone was practically burning a hole in his pocket. He'd been texting Henry on and off throughout the day but hadn't asked him the one question he really wanted to.

Damn Nathan and his stupid ideas.

As soon as he suggested it, Dom wanted it more than anything, but chances were Henry already had plans. Why wouldn't he?

Dom could almost feel the disappointment of Henry saying he couldn't make it.

Christ, this is ridiculous. I've not even asked him yet.

No time like the present.

Dom: *I know it's late notice, and I totally understand if you've already got plans, but I thought I'd ask anyway. If you're free Christmas Eve, do you fancy spending it with me? At my house? x*

He hit Send before he could second guess himself, then turned his phone on silent, set it on the passenger seat, and drove back to his aunt and uncle's house.

He managed to resist looking until he pulled onto their drive, but as soon as he turned the engine off and put the handbrake on, he had his phone in his hand.

The screen glowed bright with a message from Henry.

Dom stared at it for a second, almost afraid to open it.

Almost.

He held his breath and opened the app.

Henry: *No plans that I can't get out of. I'd love to spend the night with you x*

Another message arrived as Dom was about to reply.

Henry: *Or just the evening. That works too. Sorry, I just assumed you meant the whole night, but of course it's fine if you didn't.*

Dom laughed out loud, a smile breaking out.

Dom: *Of course I meant the whole night. I want to go to sleep with you on Christmas Eve and wake up with you Christmas morning. That okay?*

He mentally crossed his fingers.

Henry: *Yeah, I'd really like that.*

Dom smiled so wide his cheeks hurt.

Dom: *I finish at midday. I could pick you up on my way home?*

Henry: *I've got the day off. But I'd better drive myself. I need to be back in Bristol for Christmas lunch with Ella, my parents are coming down.*

Dom: *I can bring you back.*

Henry: *Don't be daft. It's miles out of your way, you don't need to be doing a 2 hour round trip on Christmas Day.*

Dom stared at his phone, nose scrunched up. Henry had a point, but he'd been looking forward to picking him up. But then if he had to take Henry home, they'd have to leave earlier for Dom to get back in time.

Dom: *Yeah, ok. Let's do that.*

Dom sent Henry his address, still smiling like an idiot. If he went into the house like this, they'd think he'd been at the whisky.

Henry: *I'll see you Friday then. x*

Dom: *Yeah. Can't wait. x*

Before he got out of the car, he sent a quick message to Nathan.

Dom: Thank you for your suggestion. I now have better plans on Christmas Eve.

The eggplant emoji he got in return had him laughing and shaking his head, but Nathan wasn't wrong.

Roll on Friday.

***

DOM'S HOUSE was pretty much exactly how Henry had pictured it. A cute two-bedroom property set a bit back from the road and surrounded by way more land than you'd get in the city.

The garden was immaculate—not that he'd expected anything less—and Henry smiled at the Christmas tree standing proud out the front of the house, covered in white fairy lights. They twinkled in the darkening sky making the cottage look almost like a Christmas card. All it needed was a blanket of snow.

A large wreath hung on the front door, thick with holly and pinecones, and finished off with a huge red bow. Henry glanced up, half expecting to see mistletoe above him and was a little disappointed when he found nothing there.

The door opened as he was still staring upward, and Dom cleared his throat, startling him.

"What are you looking for?" Dom frowned, following Henry's gaze to the top of his door.

"Mistletoe." He waved a hand at the door, then the tree. "You have everything else."

"Come here." Dom tugged on the bottom of Henry's coat, urging him inside and shutting the door behind him. "Look up."

Henry did as he was told, grinning in delight when he saw a sprig of mistletoe taped to the ceiling above them. "Would you look at that."

"You know what that means, right?" Dom murmured, stepping closer until he had Henry backed against the door.

"That you've been harassing everyone who's knocked on your door?"

Dom barked out a laugh. "I only put it there half an hour ago."

Henry wrapped his hands around Dom's waist. "For me?"

"Mm-hmm."

"Well, we don't want any bad luck, do we." Henry licked his lips and Dom's eyes darkened.

"Definitely not."

The kiss started off soft, but four days was a long time. They hadn't sexted after that first time, and Henry had thought of nothing else but this moment ever since Dom had asked him to come over.

Dom's hands were in his hair, his tongue sweeping into Henry's mouth, and thank god they were alone because the moans escaping Henry weren't quiet.

He held on for dear life as Dom pressed against him, pushing their hips together, and the unmistakable hardness in Dom's jeans sparked a fire inside him.

"Happy to see me?"

Dom's breathless laughter tickled his neck, and Henry shivered. "Can you tell?"

"Little bit." Henry ground against him, making them both moan.

"Maybe not so little, eh."

Henry grinned, loving how easy this was. "It's been a while, I can't remember."

"Oh, it's like that, is it?" Dom drew back to look at him, eyes alight with a mixture of heat and amusement.

Henry's favourite combination.

He took Henry's hand and led him towards the stairs. "I had plans of showing you around, then spoiling you with delicious food, but I see we need to get something out of the way first."

"And what's that?" Henry asked, following Dom up the stairs and staring shamelessly at his arse in those tight jeans he wore.

"I need to jog your memory." He stopped on the landing and turned to face Henry, one hand palming the bulge in his jeans. "Fuck you so hard, you don't forget again."

Oh.

Henry froze on the top step, mouth dry, pulse racing, eyes glued to the slow, teasing movement of Dom's hand on his cock. "Um . . . yes. That should do it."

Dom's laughter filled the space around them, and Henry couldn't bring himself to be embarrassed about his inadequate response. Not when Dom looked at him like that. Like Henry was the only thing that mattered in the world at that moment.

Being the sole focus of Dom's attention was a heady feeling and he grabbed onto the bannister rail to ground himself.

"Come on," Dom murmured, voice a little rough. "Let me at least show you my bedroom."

Henry took his hand again and let Dom lead him into the only room he was interested in right now. Though it could've been painted pink with gold stars and Henry still wouldn't have noticed.

All he saw was Dom.

They undressed in silence.

That was until Henry got distracted watching Dom slide his boxers down those thick thighs dusted with dark blond hairs. A low moan escaped him and he licked his lips, totally forgetting about his own boxers still halfway on, thumbs tucked into the waistband.

Dom glanced up and smiled, that soft smile that sent Henry's heart racing. "Let me help you with those." He put his hands over Henry's and slid his underwear down until they pooled on the floor at his feet.

Dom shuffled closer.

They weren't touching, not quite, but Henry's every nerve ending tingled, anticipation pulsing through him until he couldn't stand it any longer and took that final small step.

The moment they were skin to skin, Henry sighed. This was what he'd been missing, what he'd craved since the second they'd parted ways in that car park.

He wrapped his arms around Dom's neck and drew him into a kiss, lips soft and warm as they opened for him. Henry moaned, his tongue finding Dom's, turning the spark of desire in his belly to a roaring flame. Their skin touched from chest to thigh, the brush of Dom's cock against his made his breath catch, but it wasn't enough.

Nowhere near enough.

Henry wriggled a hand in between them and curled his fingers around them both. Pressed together like that, every little thrust of Dom's hips made his pulse race.

So much better.

"I've missed this." Dom muttered the words against Henry's skin, trailing kisses down his throat.

"Me too." His breath caught when Dom nipped him, the sting a sharp contrast to the pleasure winding its way through his veins. "A little too much." Henry was in danger of ending this before they'd even got started.

"We've got all night, remember."

"I know, but you had plans. I don't want to spoil any more of them."

Dom grinned and backed off, much to Henry's relief, and led him towards his bed. "I did promise to fuck you, didn't I?"

"I need reminding how big your cock is. Apparently."

Dom's laughter was contagious, and they fell onto the bed, grinning like fools and harder than Henry thought possible.

This was how it was supposed to be.

Dom set lube and condoms on the bed beside them, and Henry parted his legs in invitation, drawing his knees up to his chest.

"Hurry." Henry panted, biting his bottom lip as he watched Dom coat his fingers with lube.

Dom raised an eyebrow. "You know that makes me want to take my time, right?"

"And usually I'd be totally on board with that, but I'm afraid I might come from your fingers alone, so please hurry and put your cock in there."

Dom closed his eyes on a groan and gripped the base of his own cock. "Fuck. I'll be joining you at this rate."

Henry reached for his other hand and linked their fingers, waiting for Dom to open his eyes before repeating Dom's words back to him. "We have all night, remember?"

Dom nodded, and with a deep but shaky breath, he shuffled forwards on his knees and did as Henry asked.

"Fuck." Henry hissed at the burn as Dom slid inside him. He'd let him get two fingers in before batting his hand away and begging for his cock. He only had himself to blame for the lack of prep, but as the sharp sting eased and pleasure began to take its place, Henry regretted nothing.

He wrapped his legs around Dom's waist, hand on his arse cheeks urging him to go faster, harder, wanting everything he had to give.

Each thrust tipped him closer to the edge, Dom's powerful body blanketing Henry's, making him feel both safe and hot as fuck as he loomed above him.

Sweat slicked their skin, the scent of sex hung in the air around them, and Henry clung on as long as he could, not wanting this to end. Grabbing Henry's thigh, Dom manoeuvred his leg over his shoulder and pounded into Henry with a grunt, the new angle hitting him just right, and when Dom looked down at him, eyes heavy lidded and filled with so much want and need, he couldn't hold back any longer.

Head pressed back into the pillow, he gripped his cock and came two strokes later s they probably heard outside, his other hand gripping Dom tightly as his dick pulsed between them, coating them both.

Dom fucked into him hard, once, twice more before shuddering above him, then collapsing on top of him as his arms gave way.

It took a moment for either of them to get their breath back. After Dom rolled off him and disposed of the condom, he snuggled back into Henry's side and reached for his hand.

"Now we've got that out of the way. How about a shower, then food, and I'll show you the rest of my house?"

Henry smiled at him, still a little awed that this was his life now. How things could change in a week. "That sounds perfect."

They showered, they ate, and true to his word, Dom gave Henry a tour of his house. Unsurprisingly, Dom had a beautifully decorated tree in his living room, and they ate dinner on the sofa under its flickering fairy lights.

Henry couldn't remember enjoying a Christmas Eve more. Well, except maybe when he'd been little and obsessed with presents. But this definitely ranked up there with the Legolas on a horse he'd got when he was eight.

"Hey." Dom nudged him, and Henry smiled as Dom's hand found his. Holding hands seemed to be one of his favourite things, and it made Henry all warm inside. "I have a bottle of champagne in the fridge. How about we take it upstairs?"

Henry raised an eyebrow. "Are you trying to get me drunk, because you know I'm a sure thing, right?"

Dom laughed softly. "Oh I know how easy you are." He grunted when Henry elbowed him and smirked at him, that playfulness back in his eyes. "It's almost midnight and I wanted to celebrate our first Christmas morning together. But I also know I'll want to get you naked sometime soon, and I thought we should combine the two."

Henry nodded, struggling to find words as Dom's sank in.
Our first Christmas.
That implied there would be more, that he was already thinking ahead.

When he finally found his voice, it was way rougher than normal. "I like the sound of that." All of it.

After turning off all the lights and locking up, Dom grabbed the bottle and glasses from the kitchen and once again took Henry upstairs to his bedroom.

Of course, as soon as they were naked, they couldn't keep their hands to themselves. One blow job later and Dom coming all over Henry's chest, they finally opened the bottle of champagne.

Henry gave himself a half-hearted clean up with his discarded T-shirt, and when they were safely under the warmth of the quilt, Dom poured them each a glass, then set the bottle on the bedside table. As the time on their phones flicked over to midnight, he clinked his glass against Henry's and whispered, "Merry Christmas."

"Merry Christmas."

Henry leant in to kiss him. He tasted of bubbles and happiness and Henry wanted to stay in that moment forever. Then a thought occurred to him, and his brow furrowed.

Dom smoothed out the lines with his finger. "Why the frown?"

"Should we have got each other a present?"

Dom laughed and moved his hand down to rub at the dried flakes of come on Henry's chest. "You've been a bad, bad boy, Henry. No presents for you."

"Pretty sure I've already got everything I wanted." The words just slipped out, and Henry froze, hoping he hadn't just ruined everything.

Dom's intense gaze bored into him, and Henry took a quick sip of champagne to steady his nerves. "Do you mean that?"

"Yes." They hadn't known each other long if you counted in weeks, but Henry felt closer to Dom than he ever had Kyle. That gut feeling he ignored sometimes told him that this was *right*.

They were *right*.

And this time he was going to listen.

Dom set his glass down, so Henry did the same. "I'm sorry I didn't trust you enough to give us a chance at first." He took Henry's hand in his and twined their fingers.

"It's okay." Henry leant in and placed a soft kiss on Dom's lips. "You had your reasons, and we got there in the end."

"We did." Dom chuckled then, shaking his head.

"What?"

"I was just thinking that we didn't have a no-strings Noel after all."

"No we didn't." Henry lay back down and pulled Dom with him, hands still clasped. "And I'm so fucking happy about that."

"Me too."

Henry fell asleep with Dom's arm slung over his waist and Dom cuddled up behind him.

Just like he'd promised.

EPILOGUE

ONE YEAR LATER

"I can't believe I let you talk me into this. *Again,*" Henry grumbled as he and Dom sidestepped their way up to the first platform on the aerial walkway.

"This was your idea. Just like it was the first time we did this." Dom joined him on the platform and nudged him in the ribs. "And I told you *both* times I would've been fine doing it on my own."

Henry flashed him a bright smile, only a little forced, as he clung to the trunk of the tree. "I'll be fine once I get into it."

He so wouldn't.

Fuck, why did I think this was a good idea?

But Henry had a plan, and where better to execute it than up in the trees fearing for his life. He rolled his eyes at himself and, taking a deep breath, prised his fingers out of their death grip on the tree.

Two youngsters skipped across the walkway in front of them, making it look easy. Of course they did, because Henry seemed destined to follow after the bravest children in the world. No hugging the tree trunks for them. Henry watched in muted horror as they leant back over the edge, laughing as their dad told them to pack it in.

"All right?" Dom asked, rubbing a hand along his back, and Henry nodded.

"Yep, never better."

"Sure?" Dom darted in to give him a quick kiss, and Henry smiled, a real one this time.

It was a beautiful, clear and crisp winter's day. He couldn't have asked for a better backdrop to what he had planned. "Yeah, I'm good."

He took his turn over the wooden planks that swayed with each step. Henry gritted his teeth and ploughed ahead, determined not to let anything get to him today. He had much bigger things to be nervous about than pesky bridges between trees.

As they made their way along the course, Henry's mind drifted back to the last time they'd been in this position. He'd wanted Dom even then, knew one week wouldn't be enough for him, but their relationship had faltered, the foundations not strong enough to translate into the real world.

But they'd muddled through it anyway, getting to know one another in more than a physical way. And now their foundations were stronger than ever, and Henry couldn't remember being this happy.

"You still okay to have Luke and Nathan round for Christmas Eve?" Dom asked as he hopped from plank to plank like a gazelle out on the plains.

"Yeah, I'm looking forward to it." Christmas Eve was tomorrow night, and although it wouldn't be their first Christmas together, it'd be the first one they'd spent living together. And Dom's friends were great. They'd taken Henry in and treated him like he'd been a part of their group for years.

Dom joined him on the platform, grin a mile wide and breath visible in the chill air. They'd been living together for four months now, but Henry still had to pinch himself sometimes that this was his life.

He no longer shared a house with his mates, instead with the man who'd stolen his heart almost a year ago to this day. And okay, he still didn't have his dream job, but after a lot of soul-searching Henry had decided on a new career path and now studied to be a primary school teacher. Much to the amusement of his sister.

"You know what we should do when we get home?"

"Fuck?" Henry said without thinking, and then groaned when he saw Dom's eyes widen as he stared over his shoulder. Arse, who had he offended now?

Then Dom broke out into a grin. "Gotcha. There's no one there."

Henry slapped him on the arm. "Oh my god, I hate you."

"Nope." Dom reached for his hand, linking their fingers, eyes twinkling as he leant in close. "Pretty sure you told me you loved me just this morning." He rubbed his thumb over the back of Henry's hand, and with the way he was looking at him, Henry felt his dick stir in response, which was so not a good thing while wearing a harness.

Huffing out a put-upon sigh, he replied with, "Fine, I do love you. But only because you're pretty."

"I am pretty." Dom batted his eyelashes, and Henry laughed. "And I love you, too."

If they were anywhere other than up in the trees, he would've pulled him in for a kiss. He settled for squeezing Dom's fingers instead.

The jump between platforms was next, and unlike last time they did this, Henry hopped over without needing a pep talk first, and Dom whooped in delight. Henry's triumphant grin lasted all of ten seconds until he turned to face the next obstacle and stopped in his tracks. "What the fuck is that?"

It had to be new. Henry definitely would have remembered

walking over *that* last year. All the other walkways had a rope running waist height that you could use for balance if necessary.

This one had nothing.

Of course he'd still be attached to the overhead one by his harness, but that was it. He'd have to make his way across with nothing to hang onto if he stumbled.

Fuck.

This next walkway was the one before the netting they climbed to get to the zipwire platform. The one where Henry's plans would come to fruition. He couldn't *not* do it.

Dom came up behind him, his front brushing against Henry's back, hand resting on his hip. "You can do it. You haven't used the rope on the last two we've crossed. You don't need it."

"But I like knowing it's there if I do." Henry scowled at the offending planks of wood. They weren't even laid out nicely, but in some stupid cross formation. "*Why?*"

Dom laughed softly. "Come on, you've got this."

Well, I've no fucking choice if I want to do what I came on this stupid thing to do.

With legs like jelly and his heart threatening to burst out of his ribcage, Henry took a tentative step out onto the first plank.

It started to sway and he froze in place.

Can't do it. Can't do it. Can't do it.

"We should get a cat?" Dom said, snapping him out of his head.

"What?" Henry glanced back over to him, quickly deciding that was a bad idea when he wobbled again.

"One with attitude."

Henry snorted. "All cats have attitude." He took another tentative step when Dom spoke again.

"We could visit the local shelter after Christmas and pick one."

"Just one?" Henry said dryly. "You wouldn't want her to be lonely."

"Fine, two then."

A flicker of excitement replaced the nerves overtaking his body and Henry smiled. He loved cats. Had wanted one of his own ever since his parents had moved back up north, taking their two with them. He took another step, gasping in surprise when he realised he was already at the next platform.

Turning back to watch Dom work his way across, Henry frowned. "You said all that to distract me?"

"It worked, didn't it?"

Oh.

"You weren't serious, then?"

Henry started to climb up the netting, trying to shake the disappointment threatening to creep in, that was the last emotion he wanted to be feeling right now.

Dom's hand on his arm stopped him. "I was serious. I've been meaning to ask you for a while now."

"Oh. That's great. I love cats." Henry's smile was huge and he started climbing quicker, eager to get to the top now. "And there's something I've been wanting to ask you too." Henry reached the top of the platform and nodded at the instructor waiting for them.

He offered Henry a wink in return.

As Dom climbed up after him, Henry took a deep breath, pulled the small box out of his zip pocket, and dropped to one knee.

Dom stared down at him, eyes wide and lips curving up into a grin.

"Dominic Spencer, I love you and I want to spend the rest of my life loving you." Henry smiled up at him. "Will you marry me?"

"I'd be honoured." Dom hauled him to his feet and wrapped him in the tightest hug that their harnesses and ropes would allow. A chorus of cheers and whistles sounded behind them, and Henry's cheeks flamed.

Okay, so he hadn't counted on their slot being full and doing this in front of an audience.

But he wouldn't change it for the world.

"Congratulations," the instructor said, walking over to them. "You ready?" He gestured to the zipwire.

Henry kept his eyes on Dom as he answered. "Yeah, I'm ready."

Ready to spend the rest of my life with you.

Dom smiled, and Henry knew he was thinking the same thing when he answered, "Me too."

They stepped off the platform together, laughing as the wind whipped at their faces and their legs flailed around, and they sped down towards the last platform and the start of their life together.

ABOUT THE AUTHOR

Annabelle Jacobs lives in the South West of England with her three rowdy children, three cats, and a very naughty black Labrador.

An avid reader of fantasy herself for many years, Annabelle now spends her days writing her own stories. They're usually either fantasy or paranormal fiction, because she loves building worlds filled with magical creatures, and creating stories full of action and adventure. Her characters may have a tough time of it—fighting enemies and adversity—but they always find love in the end.

Sign up for my newsletter to receive information about upcoming books, audio and deals.

Email: ajacobsfiction@gmail.com

If you want to join my Facebook author group, Annabelle's Area, you can find it here: https://www.facebook.com/groups/798663446914946/

ALSO BY ANNABELLE JACOBS

Torsere Series:

Capture

Union

Alliance

The Lycanaeris Series:

The Altered

The Altered 2

The Altered 3

The Regents Park Pack Series:

Bitten By Mistake

Bitten By Design

Bitten By Desire

Bitten By The Alpha

Bitten By Her

Bitten By Fate

The Rebellion Series:

Escape

Defiance

Christmas Stories:

Magic & Mistletoe

A Christmas Kiss

Not Just For Christmas

Old Acquaintance

No Place Like Home

A Christmas Break

Standalone Stories:

Toy With Me

A Casual Thing

Chasing Shadows

Always Another Side

Butterfly Assassin

All Hallows' Eve

Maybe This Time

Wounded Soul